HER KNIGHT UNDER
THE MISTLETOE

BY
ANNIE O'NEIL

Published in Great Britain 2017
By Mills & Boon, an imprint of HarperCollins*Publishers*
1 London Bridge Street, London, SE1 9GF

© 2017 Annie O'Neil

ISBN: 978-0-263-92680-4

Our policy is to use papers that are natural, renewable and recyclable products and made from wood grown in sustainable forests. The logging and manufacturing processes conform to the legal environmental regulations of the country of origin.

Printed and bound in Spain
by CPI, Barcelona

Dear Reader,

There isn't a pixel of Christmas magic I don't fall for. I love it all. The lights, the crisp air (if you're in the Northern Hemisphere!), the anticipation, the giddy pleasure of buying gifts. The only thing that's better is falling in love at Christmas!

I loved writing about Amanda and Matthew— I wanted him to be a Matt, but he kept coming out as a Matthew, so who was I to argue? Amanda, who is so fiery and determined to put things right despite her wild-child past, and Matthew, whose heart is enormous but he's the last one to realise it.

Thank goodness they have the extra pixie dust of mince pies, gingerbread and tinsel to help remind them that love is the magic ingredient in seeing what really matters in life. The people in our lives.

Happy reading, everyone! And make sure you get in touch if you have any questions. You can reach me on Twitter @annieoneilbooks or on Facebook— Annie O'Neil Books.

All the best!

Annie O' xo

Books by Annie O'Neil

Mills & Boon Medical Romance

Italian Royals

Tempted by the Bridesmaid
Claiming His Pregnant Princess

Paddington Children's Hospital

Healing the Sheikh's Heart

Hot Latin Docs

Santiago's Convenient Fiancée

Christmas Eve Magic

The Nightshift Before Christmas

The Monticello Baby Miracles

One Night, Twin Consequences

One Night...with Her Boss
London's Most Eligible Doctor
Her Hot Highland Doc

Visit the Author Profile page
at millsandboon.co.uk for more titles.

Praise for
Annie O'Neil

'This is a beautifully written story that will pull you in
from page one and keep you up late, turning the pages.'
—*Goodreads* on
Doctor...to Duchess?

**Annie O'Neil won the 2016 RoNA Rose Award
for her book *Doctor...to Duchess?***

CHAPTER ONE

MATTHEW KNEW HE was making a poor job of hiding his frustration. Maybe he should have succumbed to the frivolities of the season and worn one of those ridiculous holiday jumpers to counterbalance his grim expression and biting tone.

When no answer to his earlier question was forthcoming he repeated, "You said the job was mine."

From the look on Dr. Menzies's face he might as well have said Santa wasn't real.

Ho-ho-ho. Merry Un-Christmas.

His mentor shifted uncomfortably in his chair, ultimately breaking eye contact to throw a look over Matthew's shoulder toward the floor-to-ceiling windows.

The usual buzz and whirr of the inner city A&E unit was still humming along, as if the rug *hadn't* just been yanked out from under his feet. Both his and Dr. Menzies's feet, from the looks of things. The hospital's Director of Medicine and Surgery seemed to be taking as little pleasure in the change of events as he was. Or perhaps Dr. Menzies was monitoring the progress of the Christmas decorations going up to mark the advent of the holiday season.

Tinsel, wreaths, super-sized glittering baubles and a surplus of mistletoe… The hospital's volunteer "Yule

Squad" was in turbo drive. Perhaps their powers extended to the weather. The day was cold enough for snow. But the only cloud in the sky had followed Matthew indoors and was hanging directly over his head.

Matthew remained motionless. One of his trademarks when his stress levels hit the roof. It was the only way to ensure that whoever was on the receiving end of his million-miles-away stare was none the wiser.

"As you know, Dr. Chase, these things are often more..." Dr. Menzies searched for the right word "...*fluid* than initially presented."

"Fluid."

Statement, not a question. How could the A&E job he'd been promised suddenly not be his?

"We know you have been incredibly generous—"

Matthew cut him off with a growl and a hand-swipe. He hadn't donated money for the new wing to *buy* himself the position.

"I've earned this job. The Support our Soldiers unit has nothing to do with me."

"On the contrary, Matthew, it has *everything* to do with you. You *founded* the ruddy charity. Think of the lives that have already been saved by your clinic in Sussex. And if you don't mind me saying—"

"I do." Matthew stopped him.

He knew the statistics better than anyone. Veteran suicide had outstripped soldiers dying in combat years ago. Over in the US more than a dozen soldiers were taking their lives a day. A *day*! He wasn't about to let the UK match those statistics. Not on *his* watch.

He knew the toll one of those deaths had taken on a person firsthand.

"With respect, Donald, it doesn't matter how many times the board ask me to run the unit. I am not your guy. I'm better out there." He pointed to the A&E and hoped his solid stance would draw a line under the issue.

The anonymity of the A&E was what he was after. Proximity to the SoS unit was merely…useful.

His eye snagged on a couple of orderlies wrestling with a Christmas tree, attempting to set it up haphazardly in a corner of the waiting room. He scowled. Christmas seemed to come round sooner and sooner each year. *Bah, humbug*, to it. And to the carolers who were virtually blocking the entrance. And to New Year's as well, while he was at it.

Every day was the beginning of a new year. Just not one highlighted up on the calendar with pictures of adorable rabbits or firemen.

"Dr. Chase, I think there were concerns regarding—"

"Don't you *dare* tell me this has anything to do with—" Matthew cut in, then stopped himself.

He couldn't go there. Not yet anyway. Maybe never. But at this time of year, with all of the Christmas lights, the opulently decorated trees and hordes of shoppers wrestling their gifts home everywhere he walked, it was hard not to have his nuclear family spring to mind.

Nuclear explosion, more like. Implosion? Whatever…

Either way, what was left of his family had fallen apart years ago, and a stack of plum puddings that reached to the moon and back wouldn't come close to bringing them back together.

As hard as it was, Matthew uncurled his hands from the fists they were forming. Frustration—not fury—had balled them into tight knots of steel and sinew. Okay, flesh and bone—but right now the walls around him were officially being warned. One of them would be getting a new hole if the hospital board didn't change their minds.

Dr. Menzies waved away his interruption. "There were concerns regarding your history of signing up for repeat tours…"

"What about it? I was doing my duty."

Avoiding his life, more like.

"Matthew, *I* know if you say you're going to do a job, you'll do it. I have absolute confidence in your ability. But—"

"But what? I'm used to working with mortars pounding around my medical tent. You think I can't handle an A&E in the center of London?"

Dr. Menzies gave his chin a scrub. "It's actually nothing to do with that. It's more a question of…commitment. Whether you'll want to go and work for SoS—"

"I already told you. I am one hundred percent behind the soldiers' PTSD unit. I just don't want to work there. It's not my forté. Trauma is."

Physical trauma he could deal with. Emotional…? Not so much. Besides, who would want a daily reminder of the brother he hadn't saved? The brother he had sworn to look after.

"Dr. Chase, you know I'll fight your corner until my knuckles bleed, but in this case they're bleeding and the decision has been made. The board has been clear. A monthlong job share with the other top applicant is the working plan at this point. A decision will be made as to who gets the post in the New Year. It's nothing to do with your ability. Just the usual politics."

"Politics."

The word hung between them like a noose.

Unbelievable. He'd put in the hours, the graft, the blood and the sweat. Maybe not the tears, but if he was going to come back to London for good this job and this hospital were the only reasons why.

Again his gaze drifted to the busy A&E. His pulse elevated just looking at the packed waiting room. He'd far rather be out there doing a fourteen-hour shift than standing in here talking about a job share.

Maybe "they" had a point. The management post he was trying to snag involved a lot of paperwork. And even more politics.

Something in him softened. This couldn't be easy for Dr. Menzies. He narrowed his gaze, acutely aware that his mentor had aged considerably since they'd last worked together some ten years ago. Right before his first deployment.

Matthew looked him in the eye. "Since when are we back to *Dr. Chase*?"

The question had the desired effect. The tension in the room went down a few notches and the atmosphere became not exactly friendly, but closer to how they'd been way back in the good ol' days at the teaching hospital. When learning had been learning, work had been work, and when your boss offered you a job you got it. Not had it swung in front of you like a carrot, only to have it given to another rabbit.

"So…is this how I should look forward to things working here at Bankside? *Fluidly?*"

To his credit, Dr. Menzies chuckled. The man had been more of a mentor to Matthew than his father ever had. A sting of remorse shot through him. Not that he could blame his father. Grief did strange things to a person. Especially when your one living son had done the single solitary thing he'd begged him never to do. Joined the military.

"Now, Matthew, let's not get carried away, shall we?"

"Why not?" He leaned against the doorframe of his mentor's office, having never bothered sitting down.

"Yesterday I was under the impression I'd be taking over the A&E unit in a few days' time and today it's a job share. I don't know if I need my ears cleaned, but let's see if I can remember correctly." He tapped his chin in a faux display of trying to remember the moment. "Matthew," he mimicked, expertly but not unkindly, "having you as Director of A&E would be like—"

"Butter on bread," Dr. Menzies finished for him with a shake of the head. "Look. I'm sorry, Matthew, but this one is out of my hands. You know I'd have you running the A&E this very second if I could, but…" He hesitated and looked away as he spoke on. "If we're going to carry this simile on further let's just say the candidate they have in mind would be the…er…marmalade."

"The marmalade? I'm the butter and this other mysterious candidate is the bloody *marmalade*?"

Matthew squared up to his boss—grateful there was a desk between them. Never in his life would he dream of laying a finger on him—or anyone, for that matter—but this was *news*. He wasn't here to quibble over butter vs. tangy toast toppings.

He might as well have stayed in Iraq if he'd wanted things to be straightforward. Wake up. Survive. Sleep. Repeat.

He'd come back to London to *work*. Help patients. Make sure the SoS wing opened. Maybe process a few of his own demons while he was at it. But mostly to work. When he worked there wasn't a thought in his head other than doing the best he could for the patient he was with.

Dr. Menzies rose from his chair and walked round and perched on the edge of his desk. "I know this isn't what you wanted. What either of us wanted," he hastily corrected himself, "but this other candidate has got a helluva lot of experience."

"*I* have a helluva lot of experience."

He silently ticked off the countless years of medical school, the military training, working in combat conditions. Turning his father's plastics factory into an award-winning center for prosthetics. Getting a knighthood for turning the bulk of the profits into a charity for soldiers trying to reintegrate themselves into society. What more did the world expect him to give before he'd proved himself?

"Who is he?"

"Actually… Matthew…he's a *she*."

"Job share?" Amanda's cheeks, pink from the icy walk to the hospital, turned hot and her eyes widened as the A&E department's PA raised her hands in a don't-shoot-the-messenger gesture.

"From the look on your face, I am guessing our beloved Dr. Menzies didn't make that clear? Hot tea? It's freezing out there. Or gingerbread?"

She pushed a plate of decorated ginger biscuits—stars, bells, Santas and something she couldn't identify—across her desk and rolled her eyes.

"My mum's on a mission this year to be the Christmas biscuit champion of her WI group. The weird one is a submarine. My dad." She offered as a means of explanation.

Amanda accepted a star-shaped biscuit with a smile, her eyes flicking to the PA's nameplate: Deena Stokes. She looked no-nonsense enough, even with her nails decorated like Christmas tree baubles. She also looked as if this wasn't the first time she had delivered unwelcome news to someone who should already have been in the loop.

Her dry tone intimated a certain world-weariness with her boss and his lack of communication, but her body language spoke volumes, too. She was the gatekeeper to the director's domain—and right now the drawbridge wasn't anywhere near close to landing on the other side of the moat. So it was suck it up and take a biscuit or...

"Your mum's in with a good shot if these are anything to go by."

Amanda lifted the half-eaten cookie as evidence, though with her nerves jangling round her like elves on hyperdrive even the finest pastries in the universe would taste like cardboard.

She looked toward the closed office door and tilted her head back to Deena. "I've not met with him yet. I've only had meetings with the board."

Amanda shook her head in disbelief and finished her biscuit. You had to laugh, didn't you? Just when she'd thought she'd had all her ducks lined up in a row...

"I'd been under the impression this meeting was just a formality. That the job was already mine."

Deena quirked an inquisitive eyebrow.

Humph! Looked as if someone knew better than to assume *anything*.

Rookie error. Amanda silently chastised herself for going soft in her time off from "the big leagues." If you could call raising a child and taking every locum shift in every inner city A&E on offer time off.

She shrugged away the thought. She had her Auntie Flo. And an entire floor of Flo's big old tumbledown four-story house right in the center of one of London's smartest neighborhoods. It might look like the hands of time had not moved since the first Wakehurst had set the grandfather clock up in the central entryway back in 1749, and it still lacked central heating, but it was more than most single mothers had. A *lot* more.

She parted her lips, about to ask how deep a salary

cut she'd be taking, then thought better of it. The job was round the corner from her house, in a department that brought her to life in a way no other area of medicine did. And right before Christmas beggars couldn't really be choosers. Just *thinking* of putting herself up for more overnight locum shifts made her tired.

Deena flicked her pen in the direction of Dr. Menzies's office. "He's just finishing up with an appointment. If you'd like to take a seat, he shouldn't be long."

"The other candidate?"

The PA gave a shrug, but with enough leeway for interpretation that Amanda knew that was precisely who was inside.

Amanda watched as Deena's eyes traveled from the door to some mistletoe hanging above her desk.

Hmm…

From what she'd heard, Dr. Menzies was old enough to be Deena's father, so… Her job share partner must be good-looking. She cleared her throat and sniffed. Didn't matter. She was immune to romance. Whoever was in that office was the competition, and nothing was going to stand in the way of providing for her son.

Amanda's gaze shifted toward the door. She tipped her head to the side, wishing she possessed some sort of lopsided superhero power to see through hard wood. There was the muffled flow of voices. Both male.

Most likely the old boys' club. She could picture it perfectly. A promise of the top job made over cigars and tumblers of whiskey in an exclusive members' club, no doubt. She could almost hear the tinkle of ice cubes against heavy crystal as they toasted the new Divisional Medical Director in front of a roaring fire.

She shuddered at the thought. It was how her father always did business…

So much for stuffing herself into this stupid form-fitting suit and tippy-toeing across the square in these ridiculous high heels. She should have just worn scrubs and her favorite running shoes, because from the looks of things she was going back to locum shifts at whatever trauma center would take her. The regular hours of this job would have been a godsend, but...

As per usual, it seemed that heaven was putting a hold on doling out any brownie points she might have earned up to this point.

Both women started at the eruption of a huge chorus of laughter coming from Dr. Menzies' office.

Just as she'd suspected: Old Boys' Club.

Her fingers tightened round the straps of her handbag. If she was going to go down she was going to go down fighting.

Having Tristan had necessitated dropping out of "the game" for a while. For the first three months Amanda's entire life had revolved around diapers, breastfeeding and laundry. Once Tristan had got the knack of sleeping through the night she'd started picking up shifts here and there, without bothering to take part in the "let's meet for a drink" charade. Why should she when her number one priority was her son?

Work. Parenting. That was all she had time for. Before that it had just been work. And before that...

She screwed her eyes tight and pressed her fingers to them, as if it would squish the memories away. Before that *nothing*.

She gave herself a quick shake and pasted on her smile. Another laugh sounded from the room, chased up with more rapid-fire male conversation she couldn't make out through the thick door.

Suddenly exhausted at the idea of going through the

mockery of this "interview," Amanda was sorely tempted to lean in, scratch her name out in Deena's appointment book and scarper when the door handle turned and the door opened. Two men emerged, shaking hands, clapping each other on the shoulder as if in congratulations of some sort of excellent deal made.

She didn't stand a chance in—

"Hell."

Amanda's fingers flew to her mouth. She was shocked the word had escaped her lips. Her lungs ached for air as an atom bomb of emotion detonated in her chest. And just as abruptly everything stopped. The roar of blood between her ears. The blurred vision. Her heartbeat.

Nature's way of allowing the rest of her body to process seeing the one man who had proved to her that life was still worth living. The one man who had changed everything.

Matthew Chase.

Her tongue instinctively swiped at her lips. Even from a distance she could taste him as if it was yesterday.

One part sweet to one part salty. Vintage champagne and top-of-the-line caviar, if she remembered correctly. And she had an excellent memory. Besides, her parents never threw a party that swung anywhere close to below the top line.

The third part of his taste…the spice…that had been pure, unchecked desire.

Dark hair and bright blue eyes were a personal weakness for her, and on that early spring night she had wanted more than anything to succumb. To slide her fingers into the dark silky hair just threatening to turn into curls around his shirt collar. To spend unchecked minutes gazing into his sapphire-bright eyes, trying to divine what stories might lie in the kaleidoscope of blue that lay within them.

To feel *anything*. She'd been numb for so long she'd hardly known what to do with herself.

Matthew Chase had been the first person to remind her of the spark buried so deep in her heart she'd all but forgotten it had ever existed.

Amanda could feel Deena's curious gaze on her now. And Dr. Menzies's. But she still couldn't move. She was a deer caught in the headlights of the one powerhouse of energy and seduction she had never expected to lay eyes on again.

Matthew's scent—aura, more like—was another thing altogether. And when he took a step toward her there was a swirl of... How on earth did he smell like a Nordic woodsman peeling a blood orange in the center of London? In a hospital, no less?

It was all she could do to keep her knees doing their job.

The heat blazing from his bright blue eyes struck her like bolts of lightning. This meeting was obviously as unexpected to him as it was to her.

A one-night stand.

That was all it was ever meant to have been.

It was all it had been for him.

But...

If she closed her eyes Amanda knew flashes of that night would come back to her so vividly it would be like living it all over again.

He'd seen her first. She'd known that because she'd felt his gaze on her from across the room as intensely as she was feeling it now. He hadn't just looked. His gaze had felt...*tactile*. As if he had already been undressing her. And when their eyes had met...

Fireworks.

One of those hits of recognition some people waited a lifetime for and never had. She had known that having it that night was a lifeline. A sign from above—or wherever signs come from—that she shouldn't give up. Not just yet.

She cleared her throat as Matthew closed the distance between them with another long-legged step. The whorls of heat in her chest turned into protective bars of steel. He wouldn't—*couldn't*—know about what had also happened that night.

She'd overheard enough of his cocktail party chitchat to know he was a tried and true bachelor. A determined playboy, if his one-liners were anything to go by. A committed army doctor if the newspaper headlines were to be believed. Or had he recently been decommissioned? Given himself over to the finer things in life?

She gave herself a sharp shake. Playboy or not, if he was the one threatening to take the job she rightfully deserved she was going to have play her A-game.

This was *her* job. She hadn't sat through countless interviews and buttoned herself into this ridiculous suit heaven knew how many times just to let it go without a fight.

"You two have met?" Dr. Menzies stepped between the pair of them, throwing anxious looks first at Amanda and then at Matthew.

Amanda realized that both she and Matthew had slowly been advancing on each other—as natural predators would. Cheetah vs panther? Or tiger vs lion? She'd like to think of herself as the lioness in this scenario. Ready with a killer hairdo and a roar that would knock anyone for six if they were brave enough to stick around and listen.

"Not formally," Amanda answered, quirking an eyebrow in Matthew's direction but turning on a hundred-watt smile and reaching out a hand to Dr. Menzies. "You must be Donald Menzies?"

CHAPTER TWO

IT TOOK ALL of the power in Matthew's charm arsenal to hold back a full-bodied guffaw at the Ice Queen's response.

Not *formally*?

True, he'd never learnt her name. Nor had he bothered to give her his.

But the night had been formal, all right. One of a score of similar black tie affairs he'd attended two years ago, nearly three, all aimed at making the Support our Soldiers House in Sussex a reality.

After his father had died, and his mother had hightailed it to Australia, turning the place into a rehab facility had meant the faux-Georgian mansion would be good for something. Living in it certainly wasn't.

"We met at…" He paused, drumming his fingers along his chin, feigning having to think about it.

He knew damn well where he'd met her, and how long it had taken before he had been holding her in his arms without a stitch of clothing between them. He also knew that every woman since hadn't so much as shone a light on her. Not that there had been many. One night with the Ice Queen had changed his standards.

"A charity event, wasn't it?" she prompted drily, tucking a stray strand of blond hair behind her ear before switching that diamond-bright smile back to Dr. Menzies. "Excellent places to meet like-minded people."

"For Support our Soldiers?" Dr. Menzies asked, then continued apologetically, "Of course you would already know that Matthew founded the charity if you were at one of his events."

Matthew was certain he was the only one reading the flutter of blinks masking Amanda's hazel eyes as the reaction of a woman caught off guard and quickly rebuilding her house of cards.

"It's an excellent charity," she answered smoothly. "And I have quite a few ideas about how the SoS wing here and the A&E team could really benefit by being in the same facility."

Matthew stifled another chuckle before a stark blaze of understanding wiped the smile from his face. Amanda was the other candidate for the Medical Directorship.

He'd been primed for gloves off and no holds barred—but, seeing as it was the mystery woman who'd all but set him on fire that night, this month of enforced co-working could be…fun.

His mind raced to remember if the doctors' sleeping quarters had locks on the doors.

"When was the event?" Dr. Menzies asked. "Something recent? I'm surprised neither of you made the Bankside Hospital connection."

She looked to him as if she couldn't quite remember, but Matthew could tell by the accelerated pulse thrumming at the base of her throat that she could bullseye the date as easily as he could.

"Hmm… No. It wasn't recent."

Matthew directed his gaze directly toward Amanda. He took some "thinking" time to rake his gaze along the snug fit of her suit. She was a bit curvier than the last time he'd seen her. The extra swish of hip and the ripe flush of her décolletage were…distracting.

"I'd say it was about two…maybe three years ago?"

The smallest flash of darkness crossed Amanda's composed, almost aristocratic expression. Only someone looking for a chink in her china doll veneer would have noticed.

"Yes. Something like that," she acquiesced coolly.

"Weren't you still in the military then?" Dr. Menzies directed his question to Matthew, either completely unaware of or intentionally ignoring the growing tension in the room.

"I'd recently hung up my boots."

It had actually been a year since he'd come back. His father's liver failure had yanked him back to the life he'd been trying to forget. At least he'd been there as his father had ultimately lost his halfhearted battle to survive. More than he could say for his mother, who hadn't even bothered to send a card.

The sheer bleakness of it all had forced him to make a choice. Not that the empty mansion and multi-million-pound business his father had left behind had filled the emptiness in his heart. Not by a long shot. But seeing all that misspent energy had turned Matthew's grief into a white-hot drive to have at least one good thing come from Charlie's death.

When he'd set out to create SoS he'd foolishly believed it would be the gesture he needed to pay his penance for not having been there for Charlie when he'd hung that damn rope over the beam in the attic.

The night he'd met Amanda he'd been about to close the whole SoS rehab unit down. Nothing, it seemed, could fill the void his brother had left behind. But she'd exploded his vision of the world into smithereens and he'd been trying to put it back together ever since.

Being with her had been the medicine he'd needed. It had given him hope. Proved he still had the ability to make a human connection. It had been a vital reminder that if it was possible for *him* to feel passion and loss and the sweet magic of meeting a kindred spirit, there was hope for the soldiers the new unit would help.

Not that he'd tell her she'd been nothing less than an angel that night. Not in a million years.

Turning to Dr. Menzies, Matthew went on to explain, "As you know, R&R didn't suit me so well, and my father's company needed a new direction. That's when I decided to see if we could bring SoS to London. That whole night was a bit of a blur, actually. So many new faces…"

He took his time raking the length of her again, with a look in his eye he knew wasn't altogether innocent.

High heels. Killer set of legs. Waist trim and belted, blossoming up into that inviting décolletage his fingers were itching to trace. She shifted under his gaze. *Good.* The ol' Chase charm was still working, then.

The glint in her hazel eyes was all but daring him to betray her confidence. What was it she'd said when he'd murmured into her ear that he had to know her name?

Cinderella!

That was what she'd told him her name was as she kicked off first one then her second kitten heel.

"I disappear at midnight if the Prince isn't charming."

Again, a smile teased at the corners of his lips, but holding her in suspense was far more fun than confessing that she'd all but branded herself into his mind's eye and ruined casual flings for him forever.

"So you two know each other from that event? Were you one of the donor angels, Amanda?" Dr. Menzies prompted.

Amanda. So that was her name.

She was angelic, all right… But he didn't want her on top of a Christmas tree to be admired from afar… If she were his woman he'd keep her close and warm.

"No. No…" Matthew shook his head, watching the fury build in her eyes. "I'm afraid I can't quite place you."

He dragged his top teeth across his lower lip, pleased to see twin streaks of red bloom on her cheeks.

Of course it was a total lie.

The image came to him as vividly as if she'd been taking a luxurious postcoital stretch on the massive bed they'd shared only an hour ago. Peaches and cream skin. The softest he'd ever touched. Blond hair fanned out like a halo on the pillow.

What they'd done that night hadn't been anything close to angelic. Heavenly, perhaps. But no angel would have sanctioned the charged sexual atmosphere that had lasted until well after the party had ended down in the hotel ballroom.

"Well, if it was an SoS event you definitely would have been there. And if Amanda says she was there too…"

Matthew looked across at the perplexed Dr. Menzies, almost startled to see him there.

Of *course* he'd been there. He wasn't just the founder of SoS—he was its reluctant poster boy. If he didn't turn up at the ten-grand-a-head soirées, pockets didn't open. Tickets didn't sell. And if stuffing himself into a penguin suit and making chitchat all night made sure soldiers got the help they needed—it was the least he could do.

When a person was willing to give up their life for their country the payback needed to be genuine. Especially if they felt there wasn't anything for them when they came back home.

"I'm surprised you're a contender for this job," Amanda said.

Matthew shrugged and offered her a half smile. "And why would you think that?"

"Wouldn't your energies be better placed on the new wing?"

"On the contrary." He heard his smooth tones, but knew that heat singed every word coming out of his mouth. "I think you'll find there are medical professionals far better suited to that sort of work than myself. Like at the Sussex facility—we make sure we put in proper staff so that it ticks along quite happily without me."

Amanda's lips parted as if she were about to say something else, then she clearly thought better of it. Whatever it was, it certainly wasn't about SoS. It looked personal.

"Well, goodness me. I didn't realize you were attached to the cause, Amanda?"

Dr. Menzies was beginning to look a bit desperate in his efforts to keep the conversation rolling as neither Amanda nor Matthew seemed willing participants.

"I'm not. My parents were hosting the event. I'm afraid I didn't add much to the evening's luster."

Matthew suppressed a wicked smile. Of course she had.

Twenty minutes in, one glass of champagne down, and all he'd had eyes for was the blond in the periwinkle-blue gown who looked as if a blowtorch wouldn't melt her. She hadn't just been cool, she'd been entirely uninterested. As if she'd handed her heart in at the coat check along with her handbag.

No. That wasn't it, exactly.

She'd looked as if she was hoping against all hope to forget about something. A longing *he'd* all but put a patent on since Charlie had died. Nine years and about three days before, to be exact. Not that he'd been chalking up each day since then on the walls of a memory that refused to release its stranglehold on him.

As Dr. Menzies began another halfhearted icebreaker about the weather Matthew allowed himself another slow head-to-toe scan of the Ice Queen's petite form. Her curves were shown off to maximum effect in the body-hugging power suit, forcing him to relive that night once more.

There was no forgetting the moment she'd slid the length of him, her body glowing with exertion, and ultimately thrown back her head to moan with pleasure as the two of them had joined together in a heated mutual climax. They had been a perfect match.

And now she was the competition. Wasn't life funny? And not in the *ha-ha* kind of way.

"Oh, I love this time of year. I'm always waiting with bated breath for predictions of a white Christmas."

Amanda was replying enthusiastically to Dr. Menzies stumbling comment—something about hoping the weather hadn't been too cold for her to get to the hospital.

He tuned in when the conversation turned medical.

"Ice and snow present so many different types of injuries in the A&E than in summer. Seasonal challenges. They can catch a person off guard."

She threw the final part of her comment in his direction. It was an unusual take on the holiday season he hadn't thought of. *Tis the season to be allergic to holly...*

She was no pushover. Nor was she going to let him take the job out from under her nose. She was meeting him hit for hit. Strike for strike.

Good. He loved a challenge. Especially when it had

once come in a five-foot-three package of curves and bare skin and a fabric so diaphanous he hadn't had to do much imagining to guess what lay beneath the billows of material following in her cool-as-a-cucumber wake as they'd left everyone else at the ball to their tuxedos and champagne banter.

She'd been anything *but* icy when he'd run his fingers underneath the length of the barely-there straps criss-crossing her back. Not right off the bat, of course. When one was the guest of honor at a charity event it paid to be discreet. He'd waited until the music had changed and a slow number had come on. Music more evocative of what they might be doing in bed than the feelings they would need to accompany it.

From the moment he'd crossed the room and taken her hand in his he'd known they would end up in bed together. And when all that had remained of the most erotic evening he'd ever spent with a woman was a soft indent in the pillow next to his, he'd deemed it the perfect one-night stand. He had thought there couldn't be a single woman on earth who could beat the combination of smoldering heat and pure, naked desire the pair of them had shared. A part of him had been almost sad he wasn't going to get to know her. "Sorry—manners," Dr. Menzies spluttered, shifting position so that the three of them stood in a circle. "Amanda Wakehurst…" his mentor made a courtier's bow in his direction "… I'd like you to meet Dr. Matthew Chase. Or—" He shot a nervous glance at Matthew and lowered his voice. "Do you want me to use the Sir?"

"Definitely not." Matthew gave a sharp shake of his head.

He still wasn't one hundred percent convinced he should have been given the honor. But, seeing as he'd fought wars in her name, he hadn't exactly wanted to refuse the Queen her generosity in giving him a knighthood.

"Matthew Chase."

He put out his hand and took Amanda's, pleased to feel her pulse quicken at his touch. For added impact he folded his other hand round hers, so that for all intents and purposes he was holding her hand captive.

"It is a pleasure to meet you. Formally."

"I would like to say the pleasure is all mine, but I think we both know that isn't strictly true."

At last he allowed his lips to move into a full and natural smile. "Would this have anything to do with the fact you're the 'she' who is the other contender for Medical Director?"

"You mean your job share until the better woman wins?" Amanda extracted her hand as swiftly as she could. "That's right. Consider it an Advent Calendar Countdown," she tacked on brightly. "Seeing as it's the holidays."

Matthew returned her tight smile with one of his own before she tugged her fingers away from his. One moment longer with those warm fingers of his surrounding hers and she'd be betraying her over-the-top reaction to his touch.

An accelerated pulse. The rush of heat to her cheeks. The whorls of heat swirling lazily in her belly, only to rocket straight down to a more sensual part of her body she'd really rather not be thinking about when she was meant to be at her businesslike best.

This wasn't a ball and he was *not* her Prince Charming. No matter how alive he made her feel. And if this was someone's idea of an early Christmas present she sure hoped he came with a return receipt.

She rocked back on her heels, hoping it looked as if she was giving Matthew a cool appraisal. In truth she was buying herself composure time.

How on earth was she going to share a job with her son's father?

More specifically, how was she going to put out the picture of her son she'd already had framed in readiness for her new desk and not have Matthew recognize those blue eyes looking back at him?

His name might be Tristan, but for all intents and purposes he was a mini-Matthew. Except for the blond hair. But even that was growing darker…just like his father's.

Her head was spinning from the madness of the moment. Matthew was supposed to have disappeared off to Sussex, or Syria, or wherever it was wanderlust playboys went when they grew bored with altruism. Not show up at *her* job interview!

She could hear Dr. Menzies repeating something about nothing being set in stone, that it was just an idea that the board were floating at this juncture and that with two equally talented contenders…

Ugh! It was all getting a little blurry.

"Amanda?" Dr. Menzies lightly rested a hand on her elbow and it took all her power not to jerk it back. She'd been so deep in thought she'd all but forgotten that the two men and—yes—Deena too were staring at her. "You're looking a little pale. Would you like to sit down for a minute?"

"No." She shook her head solidly, forcing herself to blank out the curious expression on Matthew's face. "Absolutely not. Just not used to…to all this heating."

"Oh?" Dr. Menzies forehead crinkled in concern.

Stop talking, you idiot!

"It's the suit. Wool. Layers."

She tugged at her lapels, undid a button, then wafted her green silk blouse away from her chest, making a little *whoo!* noise as if she'd somehow ended up on a tropical island.

"Central heating." She gave a little laugh. "Our house— my aunt's house," she swiftly corrected, "still doesn't have it. Wood burners, a geriatric range and the permanent threat of chilblains."

"People still *get* those? Where on earth do you live?" Deena asked with undisguised disbelief. "Not in London?"

Amanda couldn't help herself. She laughed. "As incongruous as it sounds, our backwards heating system is in fact the product of London in its Georgian heyday."

"Let me guess… You're a Wakehurst so…" Matthew crossed his arms and gave her another one of those disarmingly tactile full-body scans. "You live in Bedford Square."

Her eyes shot wide open. How did he—? What sort of game was he playing?

Or maybe it was just the age-old tag of being a Wakehurst. The Wakehurst name went hand in hand with central London—with stylish properties with little blue plaques indicating the people of note who had lived there—more Wakehursts—and a seemingly endless stream of fashionable soirées. Her family were the type whose titles opened doors. Nice ones.

She bit down on the inside of her cheek. It had been a long time since she'd used her full title. Lady Amanda Wakehurst.

"I've seen one of your aunt's exhibits in the British Museum," Matthew explained by way of disclosure.

"Auntie Florence?" She crinkled her forehead in confusion. Her aunt did portraiture, mostly. Some in a contemporary style, some more traditional. And usually for private collectors.

"I believe it was a collection of eighteenth-century African pottery."

"Oh…" Amanda's reeling mind quickly put together different pieces of the puzzle. "You mean my Great-Aunt Tilda. Yes, she traveled rather…extensively."

Christopher Columbus had had nothing on her Aunt Tilda. She'd been everywhere. Admittedly on the posh side of the boat…but Amanda had always likened herself to this aunt she had never known. Restless. Always trying to find her place in the world and never quite managing it.

"It would seem so," Matthew replied drily.

Amanda shrugged. She wasn't going to apologize for having been born into a family whose collections were better suited to museum displays than the bric-a-brac shelf in a family lounge. He hadn't had to grow up having to prove his worth amongst such a broad pool of high achievers. Nobel laureates. University wings bearing the family name. Heaven knew she'd spent a lifetime trying to prove herself worthy. Only to fail time and again.

Before she'd had Tristan she'd thought she might just crawl her way back into the good books via her medical career.

After she'd borne a son out of wedlock to a man she refused to name her parents had made it clear she never would be a "true" Wakehurst.

"You don't strike me as the pottery type."

Amanda knew it was a lame riposte, but she was clawing for purchase after being casually hip-bumped off the edge of a cliff. Matthew was so calm and in control, and all *she* could think about was just how throaty a groan he'd given when she'd treated first one and then the other of his nipples to hot, swift licks, chased up by tiny nips of the teeth and then kisses as she'd worked her way down that broad, steely chest of his to more...southern climes.

"How very astute."

Matthew's smile seemed to suggest he knew what she'd been thinking—which only made turning off the hedonistic thoughts more difficult. She might as well hand him the job on a platter. But she needed it more than he did. Needed the money to raise *his* son.

"I was at the museum to see an exhibition of Greek and Roman medical instruments. The only route to get there was through your aunt's collection, so I had no choice."

Amanda bridled. Was that his way of saying, *You might have had your wicked way with me once, but never again, my sweet*? Fine! She wasn't interested in revisiting that night either. Not by a long shot. Just because being in the same room with the man was wreaking havoc with her nervous system...

Oh, pish-tosh to him! It was hardly as if her family had put the exhibit in the way of his precious ancient scalpel display on *purpose*.

"Aunt Tilda was the family pariah," Amanda quipped.

Just like her. It wasn't as if announcing her "unsuitability" as a Wakehurst would make a difference to any of the labels Matthew had already lacquered her with. *Titled. Privileged.*

If only he knew how far she'd fallen...

"Sounds like you admired her...spirit." Matthew's lips twitched into a smile as she shifted uncomfortably under his gaze.

"There's nothing wrong with taking your own path!" *Whoops*. Her lips thinned as she swallowed back the rest of her retort.

The crease between Matthew's brows deepened into

a single furrow, then smoothed. "That's not quite how we see things in the military."

She *knew* how they saw things in the military. Black and white. Just like her parents. Just like John.

A hit of acid shot up her throat. *Best not go there.*

Dr. Menzies was watching the pair of them with the intent interest he might give the final match at Wimbledon. Deena was being even less subtle. And was a few steps behind in the conversation.

"Your auntie has things in the British Museum?"

"Yes. My great-aunt. She was…she was a unique character. I really admired all the things she achieved. Especially given she did it without the support of her family."

She gave herself a mental high five. She'd come this far without the support of her family, and when things got tough She channeled her great-aunt for inspiration.

Amanda had found the stories about her completely thrilling. A Victorian Adventuress, she'd called herself. A complete madwoman, according to her parents. Much the same thing they called Auntie Florence, who had inherited Tilda's house when she'd decided to become a painter, and now, of course, Amanda also bore the moniker of madwoman after her…colorful youth.

Using her trust fund to fly to Las Vegas for the weekend only to end up married to "a bit of rough" from the East End of London had definitely *not* been one of her better decisions.

It would have been fine if he'd loved her. But discovering her new husband's affection had worn off precisely at the moment she told him her parents had cut her off financially had come as a blow. He hadn't been able to find enough words in the dictionary to let her know how useless he thought she was.

When she'd spat back the same sentiments to him,

the soldier in him hadn't been able to sign up for another tour fast enough.

"Better to fight for freedom than to live with a ball and chain," he'd said as he'd slammed the door shut, duffel bag slung over his shoulder.

And she had laughed. *Laughed*.

When she'd been made a widow at the ripe old age of twenty-one everything had changed.

It had been as if each particle of joy that had lit her up inside had been switched off. Even more so when she'd gone to her parents for support. Assuming she was only after money, they'd told her it was time for her to grow up. Show some spine.

Spine?

They wanted spine? They'd see spine.

From the moment the door to her parents' house had closed she had become consumed with a drive to prove them wrong. Prove she was worth more than a mention in the society pages. It wasn't as if they'd offered her much loving support throughout her childhood. She knew her au pairs better than she knew them. There had never been a gala or dinner party left unattended on their watch. Couldn't they see how lonely she'd been? How desperate for their affection?

It was only when she'd been named the youngest doctor in Britain to run her own trauma unit that she had been ushered back into the Wakehurst fold. And that was how she'd found herself at the party that night with Matthew.

And a few months later, when she'd begun to show, she'd gone straight back to being persona non grata.

Illegitimate children did that to a family whose raison d'être was ramming a wedge between the privileged and pretty much the whole of the rest of the world who weren't lucky enough to have been born with the right surname. How her mother could never see that it was just dumb luck to be born into a life of privilege…

"So!" Matthew clapped his hands, jarring her back to the present. "Was I right? *Is* this chilblain-inducing home of yours in Bedford Square?"

She gave him a quick nod. If she wasn't mistaken, he was putting a bit more emphasis on the "bed" than the "ford." Cheeky so-and-so.

Unbidden, an image of the pair of them, completely naked and pressed together as if their lives depended upon it, burnt at the frayed edges of her reserve of cool, calm and collected.

"Good guess," she replied as neutrally as she could. "It's really convenient for the hospital. Just a hop, skip and a jump!"

She smiled brightly at Dr. Menzies, then turned to give Matthew a let's-see-what-I-can-figure-out-about-you scan—before stopping herself midway because the man was just too damn sexy for words. He was six-foot-something. She'd fit easily under his chin. Not that she imagined being in a nestling hug with him or anything… One that would feel so protective, with those strong arms wrapped round her, that wall of chest assuring her that everything would be all right. Promising that her son would always be looked after… *Their* son.

Again she found herself lost for words as she stared into those beautiful blue eyes of his.

How am I going to tell him I am the mother of his child?

"Matthew, here, has a short journey too," Dr. Menzies contributed, clearly oblivious to the frisson between his pair of would-be directors. "Just across the river—isn't that right, Matthew?"

Matthew shot the doctor a difficult to discern look. One that probably said the same thing she'd felt when Matthew all but heat-detected her bedroom in Bedford Square: *Back off.*

She liked her privacy and it looked as if he did, too. So they had that in common.

And their son.

Amanda's fingers swept along the outside pocket of her handbag, where she still kept the grainy black and white image of Tristan's first scan.

After her husband's last deployment… Well, it had been hard to believe she'd ever feel anything again. Carrying the weight of someone's senseless death did that to a person. She'd feel the heated rage in his mother's eyes until the day she died.

She might not want Matthew Chase to have this job, but she owed him a debt of thanks. Tristan meant the world to her. His arrival had let her see the good things in life again. The simple things. The sun coming up every day. The moon. The stars…when you could see them. Sapphire-blue eyes…

She'd never once pictured herself being a mother before that night, but now she couldn't imagine life without her full-of-beans toddler. Which meant she'd better get her act together and start behaving as if she wanted this job. And, no, she *wasn't* going to play nicely. She didn't want to share.

She was more than capable of running the hospital's A&E department on her own, and was prepared to prove it. Even if it meant getting a lump of coal in her Christmas stocking. From the bespoke cut of Matthew's suit, he didn't look as if he needed the money. But from the fire in his eyes he was no pushover.

She put out her hand again and gave Matthew's a short,

sharp shake, ignoring the spray of heat shooting up her arm as she turned her full attention to Dr. Menzies.

"I believe you and I have an appointment?"

"That we do, my dear, that we do."

She threw a look over her shoulder as they entered the older doctor's office and felt just the tiniest bit of smug satisfaction to see that Matthew was still watching. Hands resting on hips. Head shaking as if he'd just been diddled out of his last pound coin.

She might not want his money, but she definitely wanted this job. It would mean a regular schedule, money to pay for a proper nanny and give her sainted aunt some more time for her art, and a chance for her to rediscover the woman she had been trying to become all those years ago. A good, honest, hard-working Wakehurst.

Maybe seeing Matthew was a sign. A portent of good things yet to come. Like a job.

She dropped him a wink and swung the door closed with a light swoop of her foot. *Better luck next time, pal.*

CHAPTER THREE

"THANK YOU SO much for your time." Amanda gave Dr. Menzies a final handshake and smiled as he opened the door and they entered the waiting area outside his office together.

It had been magicked into a Christmas grotto while they'd been talking.

"Gosh, you've been busy decorating. Oops…" She held out a hand as Deena stretched up to the ceiling, one foot on her desk, the other lifting to an invisible step. "Need a hand?"

Deena looked down from the desk and shook her head. "No, thanks. I think I've got the final bit of tinsel attached now. It's Christmas or bust from here on out. Never met a holiday I couldn't decorate the living daylights out of. Everything all right, Dr. Menzies?"

She shifted gear into secretary mode as fluidly as if standing on top of her desk was the most normal thing in the world.

"Yes, wonderful."

He reached out a hand and helped her step down on to her chair and then the floor. A well-practiced routine, from the looks of things.

"Dr. Wakehurst and I have had quite the discussion."

Amanda tried to contain her satisfied smiled. Santa Claus *had* come to town after all.

She had never been one to toot her own horn, but she knew she'd killed it in the interview. She'd hit every bullet point she'd prepared and then some.

It had taken her a minute or two to compose herself after that completely out-of-character wink she'd given Matthew Chase to send him on his holly-jolly way, but having the A&E buzzing behind Dr. Menzies the entire time they'd been talking had been all Amanda needed to get back on track and strike all the right notes in the course of her interview.

Something in her belly tingled. As if seeing Matthew had emboldened her rather than disarmed her. Hmm… She might as well throw her hat all the way into the ring.

"If it's all right, I'd love to start with a few shifts down in the 'the pit' as one of the team before this job share situation kicks into action."

"Isn't that funny?"

The voice might have come from behind her, but Amanda didn't need to turn around to figure out who it belonged to. The smooth baritone was slipping down her spine as sensually as his hands had…taking their time… trailing along her back until they reached her dress's zip… which hung just above the swoop of her derriere…and then—*whoosh*. No more dress.

"I was just going to suggest the same thing."

Matthew stepped to Amanda's side, eliciting a rush of goose pimples from her fingertips straight to the top of her head.

"Great minds, eh, Ms. Wakehurst?"

He turned to her, compelling her to meet his bright blue eyes.

"Apologies. I didn't catch it the first time round. Is it Miss or Mrs.?"

"Doctor," Amanda answered solidly.

Matthew smiled. She could see he'd heard the message. It was none of his business.

"Ah! Well, then…"

Dr. Menzies's anxious demeanor returned as he eyed the pair of them. Two hungry jungle cats in the same room was never a good idea.

He drew his finger along his shirt collar and cleared his throat. "We are, of course, still finalizing exactly how this will work, and we hope to have everything solidly in place before the New Year. As I said—we've not entirely worked out the particulars. Perhaps in a week's time…when we've had a moment to sort out schedules."

"I'd just as soon start now," said Amanda, realizing as she spoke that Matthew was saying pretty much the exact same thing. "Happy to work through until a decision is made."

Swot.

Hmm…

She guessed she was too. But, unlike *Sir* Matthew, she had bills to pay.

Amanda gave him a sidelong glance, only to have her gaze clash with the same color sapphire-blue eyes she saw as she tucked Tristan into bed every night. Her eyes widened as she watched him drop her a slow, black-lashed wink. His version of a *touché*, she supposed.

Deena cleared her throat. "We've got a lot of holes to fill in the roster, Dr. M. All the way up to Christmas and through until the New Year. Matron's been threatening to call every locum in a two-hundred-mile radius and blow next year's budget if you—"

"Yes, good. Right. Okay…" Dr. Menzies opened his

palms and began to spread his arms open, as if that settled the matter.

Deena continued almost playfully. "Shifts available right now, Dr. M. Matron says Dr. McBride's head is about to start spinning if he doesn't get more help."

"Ah, yes. Dr. McBride *has* been shouldering quite a lot of extra work lately…" Dr. Menzies shot a concerned look down to "the pit."

Amanda shifted uncomfortably. Of course she was keen to work, but she hadn't meant *right now.*

She began to craft a silent conversation with Auntie Florence, begging the four millionth favor since Tristan had been born. She knew her aunt didn't mind. *Much.*

But she was over sixty now, and even though she hadn't said a word she'd noticed Florence had been going to bed earlier for the past week or two. Besides, she hardly wanted her aunt's life to be consumed by the fact her wayward niece had had a son out of wedlock and sought refuge with her, rather than crawl back to her parents and beg forgiveness.

A lifetime of living under her parents' judgmental gazes? *Unh-unh.* She'd had it from both ends of the spectrum, and refused to let anyone who supposedly "loved" her judge her again. Love should be love. And it should not come with a rulebook.

"Seeing as the lie of the land is pretty frenetic…it probably *would* be a good idea for the both of you to get a feel for the hospital. See how the place ticks."

Dr. Menzies glanced unnecessarily to the steady flow of doctors, nurses and patients one floor below them, then abruptly focused in on Amanda.

"Will this short notice be all right for you to sort out arrangements for your son?"

Ice ran through Amanda's veins. She could feel Matthew rise up to his full height behind her. He knew nothing about her child. Of course he didn't. And Dr. Menzies certainly didn't know Tristan was Matthew's son.

"I didn't realize you were a mother." Matthew's blue eyes blazed with curiosity.

"There's no reason for you to know anything about me."

She distinctly remembered avoiding all of his questions that night, finally stemming the flow of *Who are you?* and *Where did you come from?* with heated kiss after kiss.

"I thought you two had met?" Confusion washed across Dr. Menzies's eyes.

"Not formally," they answered in tandem, tension tightening both their voices.

Plowing through the taut atmosphere, Dr. Menzies continued, "So you'll be able to arrange care for him at short notice?"

"That's right." Amanda nodded, refusing to show any chink in her armor.

Any more details and Matthew was going to put two and two together. The last thing she wanted was to expose her son to a man she knew wouldn't be interested in being a father. She knew that pain in the very center of her heart.

She pasted on her "everything's fine" face, offered them both bright smiles and said, "If you'll excuse me? I just need to make a quick call."

A kid, huh? Well, so much for a few extracurricular forbidden nights under the mistletoe with the Ice Queen.

Matthew didn't bother undoing all his shirt buttons once he'd hung his suit jacket up in the nearest locker. Just pulled the thing off in a oner. More efficient.

Just like his usual One Night Only policy. He didn't *do* relationships. Didn't really even do dating. If you got attached to people sooner or later you let them down. And he was carrying around enough guilt to bury the whole of London without adding more weight to his shoulders.

He scrubbed a hand through his hair as harrowing memories from his teens began to crowd out the racier ones he'd been having about Amanda.

He'd not had a chance to check her ring finger for signs of a permanent attachment. And she had dismissed his attempts to enquire about her marital status.

Work. He needed to get some scrubs on and get out on the floor.

December was a rough month for him. Any spare time meant thinking about his brother. Going through *That Day* with a fine-toothed comb trying to think if there was anything he could have done to stop Charlie from taking that awful final step. Every single time he found fault after fault…with himself.

Which was precisely why getting to work and proving this job was already running through his veins was vital. He hadn't been man enough then…he sure as hell was going to prove he was now.

Compared to the cases he had dealt with out in Afghanistan and Syria, most inner city A&E patients were a doddle. But this time of year meant a lot of people were weighing up the pros and cons of their lives. Taking stock. What was it the Beatles had said about all the lonely people?

He wondered if the countless suicides over the course of the holiday season ever thought of all the broken hearts they'd leave behind.

He slammed his locker door shut, willing the dark thoughts to stay in there. Hidden.

While he was at it, he might as well rip any notion of extracurriculars with Amanda off his Christmas wish list. If he had one.

He slipped his trousers off, yanked open the locker door again and rammed the dark chinos into the locker before snapping a pair of dark blue scrubs out to full length and stuffing his legs into them one by one.

Just feeling the soft cotton move along his legs reminded him of the slip and shift of the hotel sheets as Amanda had made full use of her flexibility.

He swung the locker door back and forth. Maybe she'd consider...

Slam.

Why waste time speculating? They'd had a *don't ask, don't tell* thing going on that night and it had been near enough three years ago. No point in wondering what might have been.

Besides, it might be fun working with her. Interesting to see just how much of an "anything you can do I can do better" vibe he could create out in the A&E. It would keep his mind off picturing her naked, anyway.

He grinned and crossed to the mirror, tugging his fingers through his hair, trying to put it back into some semblance of publicly acceptable. He caught a glint in his eye as he did.

Who was he kidding? *Nothing* would stop him from picturing Amanda Wakefield naked.

A few moments later and he was ready for action.

He pressed open the door leading to the busy A&E department and breathed it in as if it were pure oxygen. He *loved* this. The chaos. The constant action. The demands upon a doctor to react and react and react, because every patient was important and every patient deserved his best.

He caught the eye of a doctor putting notes on the assignments board. What was it Deena had said his name was? McBride?

He strode past a couple of elderly women sitting in wheelchairs and narrowly dodged a paramedic team running in with a man on a gurney complaining of severe chest pain.

"All the resus bays are full—you're going to have to put him in the corridor."

Dr. McBride's brow was creased as he pointed the paramedics to a spot further along the corridor. He obviously wasn't happy with the situation.

"Dr. Matthew Chase." He put out his hand for a quick handshake, then flicked his head toward the gurney the paramedics were steering to a spot against a wall as they called for a crash cart. "Want me to see to that?"

"Be my guest. We've got seventy-two patients on the list. Half of them have been here for hours without so much as an initial examination."

Matthew blew out a low whistle. Well above capacity. He'd thought it looked busy from up in Dr. Menzies's office, but maybe this job share thing wasn't such a ridiculous idea after all. Then again, the crush of patients wasn't anything he hadn't seen before out on the battlefield. Too many people needing attention, never enough doctors to help. Just like life, really. Same ol', same ol'—and he was ready to get to it.

"Already on it."

As Matthew turned toward his patient he caught a glimpse of Amanda wearing a set of pale blue scrubs and approaching Dr. McBride. She looked across, caught his eye, and just as quickly looked away. He guessed she was ready to hit the ground running, too.

He knew he shouldn't be smiling as he turned around to help the paramedics preparing to hand over their patient, but there had been something about the look Amanda had shot him…

It was game on all the way—and he was ready to play.

"Aspirin? Nitroglycerin?" Matthew asked one of the paramedics.

"Yes, mate." The paramedic detailed the amounts and then continued. "He's complaining of vice-like pain round the chest. Vomited on the way over. Ashen complexion. A-type myocardial infarction."

His eyes shot to the monitor one of the nurses was attaching to his chest.

"He was in the middle of his lunch, poor bloke." He glanced at the monitors and as if on cue the heartbeat performed. "ECG consistent with anthro!"

Matt circled round, helping the team pull the bed away from the wall, issuing instructions as he went. "Find the radiographer—anybody as long as they're staff."

He didn't know the team, but A&E crews rarely did know each other. Mostly they were locums, making two to three times what the die-hard staffers took home. From the looks of some of the baby-faced white coats bringing patients in and out of the exam areas there were a lot of freshly minted newbies on tonight.

"You boys all right to see this through?" Matthew asked the men who'd brought the patient in.

The lead paramedic raised his hands in apology, "Sorry, mate. Busy night."

And off they went.

It was obvious the man would need immediate treatment. He saw a patient being wheeled out of one of the resus rooms toward Recovery and made a beeline for it with his newly adopted team.

"Can we get some anesthetic on to his wrist?" he

asked the nurse who had been securing all the monitoring equipment onto the patient. "Do we have a name?"

"Mr. Rumsey," the nurse said, swiftly applying a topical numbing agent as Matthew prepared to insert the cardiac catheter.

"Okay, Mr. Rumsey, we're going to take good care of you, all right?"

The sixty-something gentleman nodded, unable to catch his breath enough to speak.

After a quick scan of the ECG, Matthew lowered his voice to ask the nurse if there was a free cardiac cath lab.

The red-headed man in his twenties shook his head. "There is, but there's a queue. Always is," he muttered darkly.

A sharp, solid tone sounded from the monitor.

"He's coding!"

Matthew gave the patient's sternum a quick hard rub. No response.

"Need an extra pair of hands?"

Matthew looked up, grateful to see Amanda slipping through the door.

"The more the merrier. You happy to go on top?"

She shot him a sharp look.

If he'd had time to relive that moment when she'd been starkers and climbing on top him as if he was a chocolate-covered Mount Everest he would have—but there was a life at stake.

She climbed onto the edge of the patient's gurney. "You ready with oxygen?"

Matthew nodded after checking Mr. Rumsey's airways were clear, feeling for a carotid pulse at the same time. He gave a quick shake of the head. Nothing.

"Beginning compressions."

"Ready with the crash cart?" Matthew waited until a

nurse who'd joined the team gave him a nod. "Pause for air," he said needlessly.

Amanda, had already raised her hands, saying, "Twenty-nine, thirty…" as she did so.

Matthew held the bag valve mask in place while the nurse gave two full presses of oxygen before quickly applying the defibrillator pads to the patient's chest.

"How are you doing up there?"

Matt gave Amanda a quick glance. Her cheeks were pinking up as she poured her energies into the powerful compressions required to keep blood flowing into the patient's heart.

"Hands up! Are we clear?"

Matthew administered the shock pads to Mr. Rumsey's chest. They waited in silence. Nothing.

"Compressions."

Out of the corner of his eye he could see Amanda continuing the strong, steady compressions.

"Charging."

"Twenty-one, twenty-two…"

She was quietly counting under her breath. She had a nice voice. A lovely voice. Especially when she was murmuring naughty promises into his ear.

A distracting voice.

He checked the monitor again, realigning his focus.

"Clear!" He applied the shock to the patient's chest again, waited…and a whoosh of oxygen escaped his own lungs as he heard the telltale beeps indicating a restored heartbeat.

"Good work." He nodded at the female nurse. "What's your name?"

"Julia," she said, and flushed. "Julia Mayhew."

Oh, no.

Was she flirting? Normally he wouldn't care. Would

play along, even. But feeling Amanda's hazel eyes upon him, just *knowing* her eyebrows would be raised, curious to see how he responded, he fought the urge to flash Julia his trademark playboy grin.

"Can you oversee him getting a transfer up to Cardio?"

Julia nodded, obviously a bit put out that he wasn't up for a bit of naughty doctor-and-nurse foreplay.

Matt turned just in time to see Amanda covering up a snigger with her blue-gloved hands.

"Not bad compressions for a little thing."

"Ooh…" Amanda cooed, pulling off her gloves. "Thank goodness a big strong man was there to squeeze the oxygen bag. Oh, wait." She popped a single finger over the bright pink moue her lips had formed. "I think that was Julia. Girl power!"

Though they were walking side by side, Amanda somehow managed to flick her foot up and give him a little trainer-clad swat on the bum.

Matthew grinned. *This* was the kind of flirting he was comfortable with. Playground style.

He felt as if someone had flicked a switch on the pair of them. From ball gowns to scrubs. Amanda suited the role of doctor every bit as much as she did the role of the chiffon-wearing, champagne-drinking nymph he'd held in his arms—*hah!*

You had to laugh, didn't you? It had been about a thousand and one nights ago. At least it wasn't a thousand and one *knights* ago. He might not be one to settle down, but something deep within him didn't want to picture her in the arms of another man. She was special, and she deserved someone who would be there for her… night *and* day.

"Way to hit the ground running," he said, finally extracting himself from his proprietorial thoughts. He meant it too. Not everyone could walk into a strange ER and just get to it.

"Why, thank you very much. You weren't so bad yourself," she parried.

Nice. He liked a woman who could take a compliment.

"Nothing like a busy ER to get the adrenaline pumping." She did a little jog in place, then double-stepped to catch up with him.

He gave her a sidelong look and nodded. Her cheeks were flushed, bringing a warm glow to her peaches and cream complexion.

"Is this your usual buzz or are you more country GP looking to the bright lights of London for a rush? Or. no… Wait…"

He framed his hands as if he were a film director and peered at her through the square of his fingers, resisting the urge to ask whether or not there was a husband in the picture.

"Were you a Harley Street girl? Have the hushed corridors and trappings of the rich become a bit too dull for Lady Amanda?"

Amanda stopped and narrowed her eyes. She looked more sultry than suspicious, but he could tell there were questions in her eyes. And then just as quickly she popped them open and gave a quick smile.

"I like helping people. Wherever and *whoever* they are," she added pointedly.

"You two free?"

They turned in tandem to see a harried Dr. McBride standing at the main desk with patient folders in each hand.

Without even looking up he stretched out his arms. "Chase, you've got a compound tib-fib fracture in Curtain Three. Standard slip and fall. Patient's had one pint too many—wear a disposable. Wakehurst, can you see Mrs. Whitcomb? She's the one in the blue dressing gown over in the corner, talking to Miss Parrish. Take both of them. Whatever Mrs. Whitcomb has, Miss Parrish will claim to have caught it first."

He handed her the second file, then looked up at the pair of them.

Amanda looked over her shoulder at two older women sitting in wheelchairs at the far end of the waiting room. One was knitting and the other was holding up a magnifying glass to the newspaper. The puzzles pages, from the looks of things.

"Are they regulars?"

Ignoring her question, Dr. McBride threw his hands up in disbelief. "What are you waiting for? *Go!*"

Matthew shot Amanda a look. She could potentially be this man's boss and she was getting an earful. Dr. Menzies obviously hadn't clued him in to who they were. *He* didn't expect special treatment, but Amanda oozed being a class above—and was most likely used to being treated as such.

"You got it." She rapped her knuckles on the counter to attract Dr. McBride's attention. "And keep them coming. I want to get this place cleared as much as you do."

Matthew grinned as he headed off to find his patient.

Keep them coming...

As if you could stop them.

CHAPTER FOUR

"Oops!" Amanda reached out and caught near enough the full weight of a young woman losing the battle with her high heels as she stumbled through the double doors. "Steady on."

The girl threw her head back, allowing her full weight to fall on Amanda, and dissolved into peals of laughter.

Amanda blinked, almost shocked to see how the broad daylight she'd left outside when she'd entered the hospital had turned into the dark, twinkly magic night time that was London in the holidays.

Beyond the girl's huge tumble of dark curls there were miniature Christmas trees perched on old-fashioned lampposts, shop fronts done up with great swathes of gold, silver, and the beautiful deep maroon that seemed to have bewitched all the designers this year.

Christmas! If she wasn't careful the entire thing could pass her by.

Time had raced past since she'd first donned her scrubs. They'd barely cleared the lunchtime party crowd before the after-work party crowd had started stumbling in.

Twinges of guilt tickled at Amanda's conscience. She knew she hadn't even been rostered on, but with the A&E

still filled to the brim with patients it felt as if she was bailing by going home.

She managed to steer the girl round so she could get a glimpse at the wall clock. Seven o'clock.

Late! Always late. Her aunt needed to go out to an art exhibition and Tristan would be expecting his bedtime story anytime now.

Thank goodness the house was a quick five-minute run round the corner from the hospital. Even in the heels she'd slipped back on.

She bit down on the inside of her cheek as she grappled with balancing the girl. Until she got this job she didn't have a nanny. Until she had a nanny she wouldn't be able to do the job. The single mother's double-edged sword.

As she slipped her arms under the young woman's shoulders Amanda received a strong hit of mojito breath. Rum, lime and mint. She was sure of it. It had been one of her favorite cocktails back in the day, when she'd been just like this short-skirted, sequin-dressed hellion.

"Ha-a-appy Christmassh!" the girl slurred into her face.

Perhaps not *exactly* like her.

Even so, the girl's overall demeanor was one of reckless holiday abandon. A path she herself had followed one too many times. *Ha!* Who was she kidding? The whole reason she was where she was now was because she'd taken the whole society girl thing too far and her parents had kicked her out when she'd failed to pull up her proverbials.

When she'd been a trust fund girl? *Sigh*...

There had been a lot of room for improvement.

Holding on to this near mirror image of her old self, Amanda couldn't stop a teensy wave of nostalgia for the days when all she had worried about was attending lectures and then finding the trendiest bar and the hottest guy in it.

Perhaps she had a bit more in common with Matthew Chase than she was admitting. Were they kindred spirits somewhere beneath their protective layers? His macho gadabout to her... Well, she was still working on her image. Ice Queen seemed to working for now.

She looked across to see Matthew effortlessly lifting yet another reveler off the floor and into a cubicle. It seemed the whole of London was celebrating the first of December as if it were Christmas Eve itself, blissfully unaware of the twelve-hours-plus shifts the staff at Bankside were pulling just to keep the numbers manageable.

If she and Matthew hadn't shown up...

She tried to maintain eye contact with the young woman as she righted her and held her in place for a moment so she could regain her balance. Just as Amanda was about to let go the girl leant forward and popped a bright red lipstick kiss on Amanda's cheek.

"'Tis the season!" She giggled, before realigning her features to look terribly serious. "Now, Doctor Lady. Can you tell me where I can get this treated?"

She flourished her incredibly long and very highly decorated nails in Amanda's face and waggled her fingers.

"I'm sorry..." Amanda inspected the fingers. She didn't see any bruising or swelling. No bleeding. "What seems to be the problem?"

"Isn't it, like, *completely* obvious?"

The girl's cut-glass accent became more pronounced as she widened her eyes and looked around to a group of women who had to be her friends and were now stumbling through the automatic double doors in her wake.

What was it her father had always called Amanda and her group of so-called friends? A charm of charmers.

If only they knew how meaningless it all was. Like a fistful of glitter. Beautiful at first and then...*poof*...gone with the first gust of wind.

"It's my *naaaaail*." The young woman over-enunciated the word, as if to explain it to a stupid person.

"Ah!" Amanda fought the urge to thin her lips and tell the girl to get a grip.

Instead, she put on a bright smile, before placing her hands on the woman's shoulders to turn her back toward the entryway. This was exactly the sort of time-wasting the A&E department could do without.

"There are ten-minute emergency manicures available on Long Acre, in Covent Garden. Ten pounds a pop. Far better than our team could ever do."

"But I pay my *taxes*!" The girl looked back at her friends, who all looked at each other as if to ascertain whether or not that might be true.

Amanda guessed that Daddy paid taxes. These girls were dead ringers for the group she'd hung out with. Fair weather friends.

"Your taxes go to medical care. Not manicures. Besides..." She changed her tone to one of sisterhood because she knew firsthand that preaching didn't work. "Take a look at these. One of the nurses did them."

She flourished her own hand, showing off the insanely bad "manicure" her son had tried to give her. Suffice it to say his ability to color inside the lines wasn't quite up to par yet. But he'd had fun.

"You want your nails to look like this? Be my guest. You want to look fab? Head to Long Acre."

"Seriously?" The girl blinked heavy lashes as her cocktails took their toll on her motor skills.

Amanda nodded. "*The* best. Shellac. Gel. Whatever you want." She leaned in and stage-whispered for effect, "They even do *grayscale*."

"No!" The girl's fingers flew to her mouth. "That's it. I'm not having them done here. Not a chance."

She whirled around and hooked arms with the two young women who were behind her, announcing to anyone who cared to listen, "We're off to Covent Garden, girls. Nail emergency!"

Amanda shook her head and laughed. Thank goodness her aunt was constantly on trend. She couldn't even remember the last time she'd had her nails done properly.

"Adroitly handled."

For the second time that night the baritone voice rippled along her spine. Matthew was going to have to stop sneaking up on her. Especially when every spare brain cell she had was trying to figure out how best to keep him out of her and her son's lives.

She whirled around and turned her accent up a notch closer to the Queen's. "You know how it is with us socialites."

"Do I?"

"Better than most, I would assume."

She gave him an up-and-down appraisal. There wasn't a chance in the universe he would be able to convince her the night they'd shared together was more than a one-time thing for him. He had the smooth lines, the good looks and the finesse to shake off trouble like snowflakes. The kind of man to whom nothing stuck.

Which was exactly why she hadn't hunted him down the day she'd found out she was carrying his child.

She pulled the belt of her coat a bit more snugly round her waist. "I'm surprised you don't have a tuxedo lying in wait in your locker. After all, 'tis the season to dazzle the ladies of London with your Christmas...*largesse*."

He arched an eyebrow at her, the flash of darkness crossing his eyes a direct contrast to the smile teasing at his full lips. Lips she would jolly well consider paying to kiss.

If it were for charity, of course.

When she met his gaze again she was shocked to see there wasn't a trace of humor in it.

"What makes you think I don't?" Matthew countered, lowering thick black lashes to mask his eyes for a moment, before lifting them just enough for Amanda to glimpse the unfathomable pain he masked with suave comebacks and indecipherable smiles.

His hand lifted to scrub the length of his stubbled chin. She remembered the sensation of that stubble softly abrading her belly as he'd kissed the length of her midriff, moving lower, lower in a trail of kisses until she'd closed her eyes and let sensation upon sensation take possession of her and it had felt as if the heavens themselves were exploding in her body's epicenter.

"Don't you?" Matthew asked.

She saw his lips moving, but heard the words as if on a delayed audio track.

"Don't I what?"

She had been lost. Lost in those clear blue eyes of his, trying to unravel his mysteries. Now she just felt ridiculous.

Matthew, on the other hand, seemed to be enjoying her little moment of unabashed ogling.

"Ball gown in your locker. Or is Cinderella off the clock for tonight?"

Amanda twisted her embarrassment into a coil of

indignation. "Some of us have responsibilities outside the hospital."

Where had that come from?

She *never* used her son as an excuse for anything and—*uh-oh*—from the look on Matthew's face the comment hadn't gone down well at all.

"And *some of us* are channeling all our energies into proving we genuinely want to run the A&E."

"Is that a dare?"

"No," he replied solidly. "It's a challenge."

"Well, then." Amanda tugged her coat collar round her throat in preparation to swoop out through the door. "I guess it's pistols at dawn."

She swirled around in a waft of indignation—only to run straight into yet another paramedic crew wheeling in a gurney weighted with a heavily pregnant woman.

Terrific.

She rolled her eyes and diverted her course around the gurney, knowing full well that if she were to turn around that glint of humor would definitely have returned to Matthew's eyes.

Matthew stared out at the glittering reflection of Christmas lights on the River Thames. The darkness of the flat behind him seemed to make each light outside his floor-to-ceiling windows shine brighter—as if they were leering at him. Daring him to fling off the cloak of too many dark reflections and enjoy himself.

Seeing Amanda had well and truly knocked him off course. When she'd swept into his life and disappeared as if she'd never been there at all he'd been able to handle it. Knowing he'd see her day in and day out for a month... *Dangerous.*

He'd wanted to walk into Dr. Menzies's office and

withdraw his candidacy. The only thing that had stopped him was pride. He'd already given his parents ample fodder to prove he didn't have what it took to handle any task. He sure as hell wasn't going to have London's medical elite thinking the same thing. *Matthew Chase has no staying power.*

"Look after your brother, son. Can you do that for us?"

The words chilled him to the bone even today.

His father's death had done nothing to lessen the guilt.

Nor had his mother's disappearance to the Antipodes, where he had little doubt she'd started a new life. A new family. Where no one would know that her soldier son had come back from combat duty and hung himself in the attic while they were out Christmas shopping.

Abruptly, Matthew pushed himself out of the solitary chair he'd bought when he moved in and tugged open the sliding doors to the balcony, savoring the icy bite of winter air travelling deep into his lungs.

The pain felt good against the burning ache of loss.

He lifted his gaze from the festive river's edge and counted rooftops until he thought he could see Bedford Square. His chest tightened against the swell of emotion seeing Amanda again had elicited. It was a sensation he was going to have to crush.

Having Amanda Wakehurst in his life again was just a reminder of happiness he didn't deserve.

As gently as she could, Amanda eased the curly blond head out from under her arm. She rarely slept the whole night through with her little guy in the same room now that he was a toddler, but tonight… Tonight she hadn't been able to resist that small warm body crawling into her bed, snuggling into the cocoon of protective warmth she made for him when they spooned. She lifted his small ever-changing form, growing heavier in her arms almost by the day, and walked as carefully as she could toward the next room where his toddler bed was all made up with an overindulgence of soft toys.

She had to laugh. She and her aunt didn't have money coming out of their ears, but whatever money they did get they put toward Tristan. Their little Knight of Bedford Square. Or, as she liked to call him at this time of year, the best early Christmas present she'd ever had.

Carefully, she eased him underneath his duvet, enjoying the contrast of his blond hair against the blue cotton. The same color as…*sigh*… Matthew's eyes.

She tugged her own wayward sprawl of hair away from her face and grimaced into the darkness of the hallway. It was no surprise she hadn't been able to sleep. Too many thoughts. Too many memories.

"Oh, is that you still up, Amanda, darling?"

Amanda started at the sound of her aunt's voice.

"Yes! Sorry." She clasped her hands together over her pounding heart and laughed. "You frightened me. I was a million miles away. Are you back already from the art exhibition?"

"It's past midnight, love."

"Oh! Goodness. I hadn't realized."

"Was Tristan keeping you up?" Her aunt took her elbow and steered them both toward the stairwell that led up to her aunt's studio. Her "garret," as she called it.

"No, not at all. Good as gold. As ever."

"Is it just one of those nights, or is there something in particular that is rendering a glass of milk and honey useless?"

Amanda smiled. Her aunt must have noticed the empty bottles of milk she'd set outside the front door for the milkman to collect in the morning. It was her go-to insomnia cure, but tonight… Useless.

"It's the new job," she admitted, squinting her eyes against the glow of the floor lamp her aunt had turned on.

"Sit," her aunt instructed, pointing Amanda toward a cushiony armchair that was just perfect for curling up in, legs and all. "Speak."

She grinned at her auntie, her heart filling with gratitude that at least one member of her family wasn't obsessed with social climbing. Living with Lady Florence Wakehurst, her father's sister, was akin to living with a whirling dervish. A whirling dervish who, like a rainbow or a break in the clouds, provided moments of genuine clarity and peace. She was like a lady Buddha, bohemian artist and businesswoman all wrapped into one. And she was the one person who hadn't judged her when she'd turned up pregnant and alone.

"They want it to be a job share."

Her aunt's gaze sharpened. "Oh?"

Amanda nodded. "Well. Not exactly. But sort of."

"Amanda, darling, you're being obtuse."

Amanda snorted at her aunt's dry expression. "They want me to work together with someone for the next month or so until they figure out which one of us they want. Although the director kept saying the situation was 'fluid.' Whatever that means."

"Not exactly standard practice, but it doesn't sound completely mad. They want to sample before they buy. Not to worry. You're an excellent doctor, darling. And a wonderful manager. Who's the competition? Surely you'll wipe the floor with them."

Amanda traced her finger along the curlicue design in the ancient chair's upholstery. Something Auntie Flo had inherited from a great-great-grandmother, from the threadbare looks of things.

"I could do it. I'll just never be around. And what's the point in earning all that money only to beg more favors I don't deserve from you or pay someone else to spend time with Tristan?" She lifted her hands into the air and let them fall into her lap. "I mean, that kind of defeats the whole point of having a son, doesn't it?"

"It depends upon who you ask, dear." Her aunt gave a wicked giggle then held up her index finger. "First point—I love my grandnephew, so spending time with him is hardly a chore, and hiring someone to give your decrepit Auntie periodic relief would only widen his social skills. There's also the nursery round the corner. Secondly, I know I'm completely ancient, but in my day we were all shipped off to boarding school before we could form complete sentences and not allowed to return until we could drop thrilling *bon mots* into teatime conversations. Or, in my case, make a perfect dry martini."

"Is that what happened to you and Dad?"

Amanda faltered a little on the final word. A part of her knew her father had been trying to do the right thing by withdrawing her trust fund when she'd gone off the rails. But rejecting her lock, stock and barrel because she'd had a son out of wedlock... Now, that was something she'd thought only happened "back in the day."

"Our parents were raised in a terrifically strict Edwardian household. Children were seen and not heard." Her aunt gave her long strand of pearls a tug, then swirled the tips of her fingers along her temples as if her head ached at the memory. "Not really seen *that much*, if the truth be told. Tristan knows you love him. Whatever time you have with him when you get your career up and running again will be enough."

Amanda tried to return her aunt's gentle smile, but just couldn't make herself. This wasn't the only job in the world, but it certainly was the one she knew would engage her and keep her ever-active mind focused. Maybe her father was right. She always leapt before she looked… and this time there were consequences.

She drummed her fingers along her chin. "If only there was a way to convince him he didn't really want the job."

"The competition…?" her aunt intoned playfully.

For an instant a crystal-clear image of Matthew swept all her other thoughts away. His pitch-black hair. Blue eyes that could light up a room. Or at least increase her blood temperature a degree or two. Enough alpha male pounding through his system to see him into battle and back again. Little wonder he'd become a soldier. The man was potent. If he'd been in war zones it was understandable that he had that odd, faraway look in his eyes. And not that surprising she was attracted to him.

A sting of pain shot through her. Had she used him to make up for what had happened to John? *Ugh*. If only this chair would swallow her up and let her start the day over again she would never set foot in Bankside.

"You did meet the other person today?" her aunt pressed.

"He's no one really."

Lies. Lying. Liar. He was… He was every single thing she thought she'd want in a man. And every single thing she couldn't have.

"Aha!" Her aunt cackled, pressing herself up and putting on the kettle she kept in the corner of the studio. "It looks to me as if my little darling niece is on the knife's edge of a dilemma. Come on, luvvie." She crooked her index finger and wiggled it back and forth. "Tell Auntie Florence all about it."

After a day of holding it all in, Amanda suddenly let the wash of emotions burst through her. "The 'competition' is Tristan's father."

"Ah." To her credit her aunt didn't flinch, gasp or shriek with dismay. "And I'm guessing the good doctor still has no idea he has a little version of himself running around London town."

Amanda shook her head, then dropped her forehead into her hands. What a mess!

"So," her aunt continued, pouring boiling water into an ancient china teapot, "now that I'm a bit more in the picture, it appears to me that it's not so much that you don't want it to be a job share—it's that you don't want it to be a job share with *him*."

"That's just it!" Amanda wailed. "He's…he's…*perfect*!"

And he had been. It had been as if they'd worked together from the day each of them had been handed a stethoscope and pointed toward a busy emergency ward. They'd seemed to have a sixth sense about each other. An ability to know where the other was at all times. If they needed help. If they didn't.

Exactly the same as the moment they had caught one another's eye at the benefit all those years ago. As if it had been predestined that they would be together.

Fate.

"Bad luck, darling."

Or bad luck.

Amanda sighed. "Maybe not. It's just life." He was probably laughing about their three-years-ago dalliance right now.

No. That wasn't fair. He didn't strike her as cruel. Nor

was he someone who would bow out of the job without proving his worth.

"In my experience, love, there's nothing a good cup of tea can't fix." Her aunt cradled the delicate cup in a saucer and handed it across to her niece. "Chamomile. To help you get some sleep. In the morning a solution will no doubt present itself."

Amanda thanked her and blew across the steaming surface of the tea, watching it ripple as her breath hit it. A storm in a teacup. Fingers crossed that wouldn't translate to working with Matthew. That was one storm she could do without.

CHAPTER FIVE

STILL SCRUBBING THE sleep out of her eyes, Amanda pulled the changing room door open on the ever-busy A&E, only to find herself face to chest with…oh…surprise, surprise… Matthew Chase.

He'd been just about every-bloody-where she'd turned over the past week. The only place she *didn't* seem to run into him was the ladies' room. It was a shame hiding out in a cubicle wasn't a way to turn the tables in her favor. Besides, from everything she'd seen Matthew was every bit as capable of running the A&E as she was.

Didn't mean she had to like it.

"Hello, Amanda. Fancy meeting you here."

"Mmm…" She did her best to hide the rush of goose pimples rippling across her skin by a crafty crossing her arms over her chest maneuver. As if she could fool a man like him. He'd probably *invented* all the tricks in the book. "I could say the same, but I suspect we are both operating with the same ulterior motives."

Matthew feigned shock. "*Moi?* I think you will find my intentions are purely chivalrous. Lending a hand in a busy A&E department—"

She waved a hand in front of his face. "Save it for the board. I'm not the one you need to be impressing." She pointed out to the full waiting room. "They are."

Matthew didn't turn to look. He had, after all, just walked through the crowd. Instead he stood his ground, filling the doorway like a sexy grizzly bear minus the hirsute thing. And the claws. The smile was winning enough. And dangerous enough.

Don't go there. He's off-limits and you are the Ice Queen. Just keep it on a loop. I am the Ice Queen. I am the Ice Queen.

He took a step back to allow her to pass.

See? Powerful.

"I think the board will see sense soon enough. Realize this is a one-woman job. Now, if you'll excuse me? I have patients to see."

She used her fingertips to press his chest, so that he'd take a couple more steps back. It was more of a survival move than a genuine desire to launch herself into the fray, but standing there in that swirl of Matthew's signature aroma… Mmm, this morning it came with a dash of pine needles and nutmeg. Christmassy.

How did he manage to look so…awake? Bright blue eyes twinkling, hair a bit…well…*rakish* suited him, so the mussed-up look didn't matter so much. But—sweet honey buckets—the man just oozed vitality. It was all she could do to sweep past with a supercilious air of you-don't-affect-me-at-all.

"See you out there, Cinders."

The word lodged in her spine like an ice pick.

Cinderella.

That was what she'd so flippantly called herself that night. The only thing was, there were no glass slippers hidden in her house after that unforgettable evening. Just one perfect little boy.

"Does that make you the pumpkin or one of the mice coachmen?" she asked coolly.

"I thought that would've been obvious."

Matthew's voice deepened as he turned his sexy vibes up to high. As if he had to.

"Mmm… Not so obvious from where I'm standing."

Amanda raised her eyebrows and impatiently tapped her fingers along her forearm, not a little pleased to note that her ability to lie to his face was improving. Maybe she was growing immune to him.

He leant in close and growled in her ear, "I'm the big bad wolf."

As he swept past her a shot of heat jetted straight to her erogenous zones so powerfully it was as if she'd just rolled off him and was enjoying the afterglow of a mind-blowing orgasm.

Okay. Not so immune.

But until she figured out a way to let him know he was Tristan's father she was going to have to keep her game face on.

"Dr. Chase!"

Matthew looked up from his patient notes to see Dr. Menzies entering the doctors' lounge. "All right, guv? What can I do you for?"

The older gentleman walked to the kettle, lifted it, then raised his eyebrows to ask the age-old question. "Cuppa?"

Matthew nodded, the wheels in his mind beginning to turn and whirr at high speed. Cups of tea usually came with bad news.

"I'll take the tea, but you'd better be the one to tell me whether or not I'm sweet enough."

Dr. Menzies laughed. "No need for sugar today, Matthew." He walked to the sink to fill the kettle.

"But…?"

He heard the tap stop and his mentor sigh. Felt the

air thicken as the director gathered his thoughts. Matthew was no mind reader, but he wasn't blind. He'd seen Amanda bewitch and delight the A&E crew, doctor by doctor, nurse by nurse, from reception straight on through to top administration. It was obvious she was a natural manager and an excellent doctor.

That and Matthew hadn't been deaf to the near constant barrage of questions as to why he wasn't simply helming the SoS unit—seeing as he was the man who had set it up.

But how could he look a soldier in the eye and tell him he would be there for him when he hadn't been there for his own brother?

Matthew sighed and pushed his paperwork to the side. "Shall I put you out of your misery and just say it for you? You're giving the job to Amanda."

Dr. Menzies turned around, a gentle half smile playing on his lips. The other half of his expression was, Matthew guessed, weariness at having to deal with the politics of running a hospital when medicine was really what made him tick.

"No. That's not it at all." He finished making the mugs of tea, slid them on the table and pulled out a chair to join Matthew. "Dr. McBride voiced a certain…*concern*… yesterday."

"The chap who runs the A&E sometimes?"

"Yes. Today being one of them." Dr. Menzies nodded, his eyes glued to his mug of tea as though it held the answers to the mystery of the universe. "He was a little concerned about the…*ah*…the competitive nature of your relationship with Dr. Wakehurst."

Matthew shrugged. "It's only natural. We're both up for the same job."

"True, but what if the board decides to go with making the position a permanent job share? You are going to have to get along with her. And if they don't… I can tell you which position they'd rather you took up."

A vivid flash of holding Amanda in his arms, their legs woven together as if they were one person, sharing breath and kisses, touching and holding each other's bodies with such raw desire it would have been impossible to believe one could survive without the other, shook Matthew to his core.

Just as quickly a surge of indignation wiped it clean. He didn't need Amanda. Didn't need anyone. After three tours in full-blown war zones, trying his best to understand what his brother had gone through—and failing—he could run the A&E with his eyes shut. He knew chaos as well as he knew the backs of his hands.

"What's this really about, Donald? Is it one of those ticking the boxes things? Does the hospital need more women in senior roles? Is that what this is about? Playing nicey-nicey? You should know better than anyone I'm not into politics. I'm into solving things. Fixing things. Like patients."

Without waiting for a response he closed the patient file, gathered up the rest of his paperwork and rose from his chair.

Rapping his knuckles on the table, he continued. "Here's the deal. For the rest of this month I will appear, ready to work at seven a.m. on the dot, Monday to Friday, weekends if necessary, and I will work through until the next shift is properly up and running. What Dr. Wakehurst does or doesn't do to prove herself willing to go the full mile for this job is up to her. If, at the end of the month, you decide I'm the man for the job I'll take it. If not, I'll walk away—no hard feelings. But in the meantime you can tell the rest of the team that a little healthy competition never hurt anyone. Because where I come from? Everyone's *not* a winner. And if Dr. Wakehurst isn't up to a bit of ribbing because early starts don't suit, don't hire her."

The sound of clapping came from the doorway. "Bravo, Dr. Chase. Fighting words if ever I heard them."

"Amanda," Dr. Menzies spilt some tea out of his mug as he pushed himself up to stand. "We were just discussing—"

She held up a hand and waved away whatever apology he was about to offer, her hazel eyes solidly locked on Matthew. "I heard. And that's fine with me. Seven a.m. is my favorite time of day."

"I thought it was midnight."

Matthew knew there was an edge to his voice, but the more he was getting to know this woman the more he knew he'd pinned a label on her that didn't suit at all. It was more than obvious that she was someone special. A stand-out, even. Not at all the spoiled heiress he'd pegged her to be—a woman playing the field until Daddy arranged for her to marry one of her own or bought her a clinic on London's Harley Street, full of private practices.

The fact that Matthew himself was newly titled made about as much impact on the blue-blood set she belonged to as nouveau riche did to the old money crowd. *Nada*. Not that wedding bells were what he had in mind.

Wait a minute…

Were they?

No. Of course not. He didn't do commitment. He didn't do love. He didn't do happy families. He did work. And he did blocking out the pain and getting through the days with the odd hour out to have a glass of whiskey with a colleague. Not that he'd even had time for one of those lately.

"I think we're happy to carry on as we have been. Or am I misreading the signals, Dr. Wakehurst?"

Matthew watched her take a moment. Assess him. He could practically see the wheels turning behind those hazel eyes of hers. He wasn't playing fair. She had a child to support. He didn't need the money. He just needed to keep busy, and when he'd heard about the A&E job he'd leapt without thinking.

Heading the SoS Unit—which he *should* be doing—would be just too painful. Too intense a daily reminder of men who were on the brink. Some they would save. Some they wouldn't. And it was the ones they couldn't that would haunt him every bit as much as the memory of his brother did. In the A&E they simply didn't have the time to care. Just to work.

"The seven a.m. shift suits me to a T. Thank you for your consideration in asking, Dr. Chase."

The sweet smile Amanda was sending his way in no way met her eyes. He didn't like knowing he was the reason behind it.

"Good! Well, seeing as you're both in agreement…" Dr. Menzies cut into the ever-tightening silence with a solid clap of his hands. "I'm thrilled. It was actually what I was going to suggest. In the long run, should the job become a joint position, you'd more than likely be working different hours, but…"

His glasses slipped low on his nose as he swung his gaze from Matthew to Amanda and then back again.

"If you can't work together as a finely tuned *team* the whole exercise is pointless. So, shall we say for the rest of December the two of you will carry on as you have been, with more of an eye to seeing how the pair of you work as a unit? Rather than using one-upmanship to showcase your medical skills which, as we all know, are exemplary."

Matthew sensed a growing build-up of steam in his bloodstream. This was all very playground, and he wasn't into games. He had half a mind to chuck the whole thing in and sign up for another— *Ah*.

He huffed out a reluctant laugh. Part of the test, was it? His usual remit was to cut and run to the world's worst places. Prove to himself that there were people fighting demons darker than his own. Funny how living a "normal" life seemed so out of reach. The wife. The kids. The blasted picket fence. None of it seemed achievable.

He glanced across at Amanda, busy processing the new terms and conditions in her usual cool-as-a-cucumber fashion. She looked up and their gazes clashed, then meshed. A normal life might not seem achievable. But with Amanda at his side he had the feeling the Bankside A&E was never going to be the same again.

"Right, then." He briskly crossed the room, dropping his patient forms in the out-tray by the door and rubbing his hands together before swinging the door open. "Guess we'd best get to it."

A few hours later Amanda was eying the board for her next patient. She reeled round at the sound of a woman screaming for help.

"My boy! My baby boy! Please help!"

She ran around the counter, banging her hip so hard on the sharp corner she nearly saw stars, but she heard the fear in the woman's voice and swallowed down the pain.

A twenty-something woman was holding a writhing body in her arms—an infant. Perhaps five…six months old. The swaddling was coming loose and it was all the woman could do to keep hold of him.

Amanda reached out and took the child in her own arms, scanning the area for anyone who would help.

Dr. McBride saw the situation and sent her straight to a resus room. Amanda didn't waste a moment looking back. She knew the mother would follow her.

"Let's get this little guy on his side on a gurney." She checked to make sure the baby's airways were clear. "What's his name?"

"Robbie," the mother sobbed, her Irish accent thickening as she continued. "Is my baby going to be all right?"

"He's seizing. It should pass in a minute. I know it's frightening to watch."

Amanda calmly held the child in place, checking by touch for fever and by sight for any signs of a rash.

"Has Robbie been ill recently?"

"No. Nothing. He's a healthy little boy. Smaller than most, but he's been fine."

"And you've noticed absolutely nothing out of the ordinary?" Amanda glanced at the mother, who had come round to the other side of the table. "Look—see. There we go. He looks to be coming out of it."

As the baby settled Amanda ran through a quick series of tests, including a look into the child's eyes. What she saw chilled her to the bone.

"He's not done this before?"

"No. No." The mother kept shaking her head, then stopped, her eyes widening. "He has been struggling a bit with stiffness and a wee cough, but I thought it was just growing pains."

"Okay." Amanda nodded.

That wasn't it. Babies were built to grow at a rapid rate in their first year, and she could tell just from the child's slight build that something was…*off*.

She clapped her hands, out of sight of Robbie, who was

now turned toward his mother. No response. She waved a hand just along his peripheral vision. Again, no response.

Robbie's response to light and sound wasn't what it should be and, more worryingly, when she rolled him on to his back and used her light pen to look into his baby blue eyes she saw little red dots. Cherry-red. Right in the center of his retinas.

Amanda could barely stem the rush of emotion she felt. It was rare. But she'd seen it before. Tay-Sachs disease. An incredibly cruel, genetically inherited disease that all but guaranteed the child would die before he was five years old.

But before she said anything she'd need to run some tests and get a second opinion.

She could hear Matthew speaking with someone just outside her curtain—wrapping up a case, from what she could gather. Tay-Sachs wasn't his area of expertise, but...

Not asking for help just because of pride is foolish.

This wasn't about her. It was about her patient and she'd taken an oath.

Big breath in and then she tugged the curtains apart after asking Robbie's mother to wait for just a couple of minutes while she conferred with a colleague...

"Dr. Chase, could I borrow you for just a moment?"

Matthew turned to her, his eyes widening a bit in surprise. Since their "telling off" they had been doing their utmost to avoid any interaction at all. It just seemed easier that way.

She quickly explained the situation and watched as Matthew's expression turned sober.

"Are you absolutely sure you saw it? We don't want to cause the mother undue worry."

Amanda nodded. She could tell Matthew was asking

the question more out of concern for the patient rather than second-guessing her visual diagnosis.

"Shall we take a look together? Use me as an extra pair of hands to take the blood and DNA tests. If you're wrong, you can blame the extra tests on me being over-cautious."

She gave him a smile of thanks. "That's kind, but I don't need you to fall on your sword for me."

"I know. But…" He hesitated.

Would he?

Everything in her stilled. Would Matthew be prepared to give up his lifestyle to be a father to their child?

She sought his eyes for answers, and when none were forthcoming she forced the conversation forward.

"Go on. What were you going to say?"

He blinked and smiled, as if they'd each come out of a moment frozen in time and nothing more intimate than a simple handshake had ever passed between them.

"Best we prove we can work as a team, right?"

Amanda nodded. That wasn't what he'd been going to say, but she'd take it. Far better to have their relationship amicable when he found out that the bond they shared went much deeper than…

She stopped the thought before it had a chance to form fully. This wasn't the time or the place to let him know they could be much more than a team. They could be a family.

Before she could respond Matthew was in the cubicle, pulling the curtain shut behind them and introducing himself to Robbie's mother. "Is it Mrs. O'Shea?"

"Miss." Robbie's mother sniffled. "His father and I were never married."

Matthew nodded, and rather than comment on the

information began steadily explaining the tests he was repeating—tests that Amanda had already conducted.

"Irish name, is it?" he asked, then looked up at the mother with a smile. "I'm detecting an accent."

She nodded. "We came over a few months ago and… um… London didn't suit his father."

"What? The finest place on earth?"

Matthew feigned surprise to cover up what was blatantly obvious. *Parenthood* hadn't suited the father. The defensiveness in her voice had all but spelled it out.

Matthew finished his eye exam, then looked across at Robbie's mum. "Well, that's enough of poking my light stick in poor little Robbie's eyes."

From the change in his tone Amanda didn't need to look at Matthew to know he'd seen exactly what she'd seen. The bright red dots.

"Dr. Wakehurst, I'd like to take a small blood sample, if you agree. And a DNA test as well—if that's all right, Miss O'Shea?"

"Please, call me Jenny. But…" Her expression was pained and she clutched Amanda's arm. "I don't understand why you need a DNA test. His father knows he's the dad—he's just not interested in being in Robbie's life. We're fine on our own. I just want to know what happened today."

"Nothing to do with paternity. The tests are all part of dotting our i's and crossing our t's." Matthew explained calmly, methodically putting together a tray of all the needles and other equipment he needed.

"Won't taking the blood sample hurt him?" Jenny's fingers flew to her mouth. "The poor lad's been through so much already today—is it really necessary?"

Amanda gave Jenny a gentle smile and laid her hand on the anxious mother's arm as she pulled over a small cart with the necessary supplies. "We just want to get to the bottom of why Robbie seized today. Perhaps you could hold him in your arms and give him a good cuddle while we get everything together? Babies can tell when their mums are stressed."

"It's kind of hard not to be when it's your little boy. My parents are gone. He's all I've got."

Tears welled in her eyes and Amanda strained to keep a check on her own emotions. This must be terrifying for her. All alone in London, without the father of her baby. No. Worse. Knowing the father had no interest in being a part of his little boy's life.

She knew that if she looked at Matthew now she would betray what she feared most from him. Rejection.

This isn't about you.

Amanda forced herself to regroup. If this poor baby *did* have Tay-Sachs disease, Jenny would be facing a dark future. As soon as they had the test results she would know whether or not her little boy would die within the next few years. And then she really would be all alone.

Over the next few minutes Amanda and Matthew kept up a steady stream of dialogue, explaining what they were doing, distracting Jenny with questions about Christmas as Matthew delicately inserted the butterfly needle and withdrew the necessary amount of blood. They swabbed the inside of Robbie's cheek for DNA and labeled everything for the lab.

Amanda couldn't help but be impressed by how gentle and caring Matthew was. He threw her the odd curious glance—surprised, she supposed, that she had effectively let him take over the treatment while she acted as his nurse.

He deserves to know. Deserves to know he has a child.

"Right, then, Jenny. It looks like we have everything

we need here. Dr. Wakehurst, would you like to take her to one of our private rooms to wait?"

Amanda nodded. She knew what he was saying. If the news was bad Jenny would need her privacy. For tears. Possibly screams of despair. The disbelief. The heartache.

"Good idea." She looked Matthew squarely in the eye, parted her lips to speak—and suddenly couldn't say a word.

She mouthed *thank you*, then turned to escort Jenny and Robbie down the hall.

CHAPTER SIX

MATTHEW LOOKED AT the test results and felt his stomach drop.

Tay-Sachs. No doubt about it.

He thanked the lab technician for prioritizing the tests and headed down the corridor to the lift. What a miserable piece of news to deliver. He knew it shouldn't make a difference that it was the holiday season, but his brother's death had tainted this time of year for him forever. Miss O'Shea would no doubt come to hate Christmas as much as he did.

His heart ached for the mother and her child. As he punched the button in the lift for the ground floor the unease cinching round his heart tightened. It was Amanda he was thinking of. What her reaction would be when she heard the news. How she'd deal with it. She had a child. A little boy, if he remembered correctly.

Of *course* it was a little boy. There wasn't a thing about Amanda Wakehurst he could forget if he tried. He wondered whether the father was involved in their lives, then forced himself to stop. She'd made it clear that her personal life wasn't his business, but the more he worked with her…saw the layers that made up this woman who was both complicated and purely individual…the more he caught himself thinking, *This isn't enough. I want to know more.*

The moment the lift doors opened he saw Amanda, body poised, eyes alert, as if she'd been expecting him at this exact moment. And when their eyes met she knew. She knew what lay in store for their patient and his mother.

He thought he'd seen it before. Her vulnerability. But up until this very moment he'd read the faltering in her bright smile whenever their eyes met as the competitive edge of a woman used to getting what she wanted.

Not anymore.

The slight tremor in her hands as she approached showed him plain as day that Amanda was every bit as human as he was. Fragile, even. But she wore her tough-girl attitude like a bulletproof vest. Probably even slept in it.

As his heart all but pounded straight through his chest he was shocked to feel a growing desire to protect her from anything that would dim the light in those warm hazel eyes of hers.

Wordlessly, he handed her the test results. As she processed the news he saw a complication of emotions cross those eyes of hers. Sorrow. Fear. Pain. And when she lifted her gaze to meet his he was humbled to see what shone through most clearly.

Empathy.

"She's in one of the family rooms. I'll go tell her."

Matthew reached out and touched her elbow, as if it would lessen the weight of the task. "I'll come with you, if you like."

Amanda considered him a moment, took a step back, then shook her head. "No. If the father's not in her boy's life I think she'll probably need a woman giving her the news. A mother."

For a microsecond he thought he saw her eyes mist, but just as quickly the moment had passed. She was a professional. And she would deliver the news compassionately.

He watched as she turned, the shake in her hands now imperceptible, and opened the door to explain the genetic disorder that would change the O'Sheas' lives forever.

A rush of rage filled him that life could be so cruel. So...*arbitrary*. Just as it had been with his brother. Depression in a soldier of note... A man who had risked his life to save so many others...

Matt pushed off from the wall he'd been leaning on with his heel. *Work*. It was the only way to drown out the demons.

As he passed the room Amanda was in he heard a cry of disbelief. A cruel reminder that some demons were worse than others.

"Looks like someone needs a drink."

Amanda secured the top button of her coat and forced a wry smile to her lips before meeting Matthew's inquisitive gaze. "That obvious?"

Matt nodded, his expression gentle. Concerned. "If I said I could tell from a mile away would you be offended?"

"Not really." She huffed out a deep sigh. "I can't imagine my day was tougher than any of those you had out in Afghanistan."

"I'd say it was on a par." He crooked his arm and offered it to her. "Bad things can happen, no matter where you are. Drink?"

Amanda's head tipped back as she laughed. "I'm guessing you're not going to take me to the Optimists' Club."

"Is there such a thing?" Matt tucked Amanda's hand

into the crook of his arm. "C'mon. Let's get you out of here and have a glass of—"

He pulled back and looked at her. He'd been about to say champagne, but she would hardly want to toast such an awful day with bubbles.

"Christmas cheer? I can never resist mulled wine," Amanda confessed, her expression lightening a bit.

"If you insist."

He'd gone for jocular and ended up sounding truculent. It wasn't *her* fault he hated Christmas. And it was not his intention to further dampen her spirits.

Amanda pulled her fingers out of the crook of his arm and stuffed both her hands deep into her coat pockets. "I should probably get back home. Give my own little guy a hug."

She glanced up at the wall clock. He saw her waver. Just enough to make him try again.

"A glass of mulled wine would do us both good. Give you a chance to shake the day off before you see him. Lady's choice of venue?"

He offered her a little half-bow and a hopeful smile. Going home wearing such a heavy cloak of sorrow wouldn't be good for anyone. Not that he was responsible for Amanda's happiness or anything. But he could take her for a drink. As a colleague. That was hardly pushing the boat out.

Or slipping a ring on her finger.

Where had that come from?

He was just about to tell her to forget it when Amanda's lips thinned again, then twisted into a contemplative moue as she looked at him through narrowed eyes.

What went on in that head of hers? It surprised him to note how much he actually wanted to know. Normally the less he knew, the better. But Amanda had him all topsy-turvy, and he wasn't one hundred percent sure why he kept coming back for more. Moth to the flame sprang to mind. Or was it more like two peas in a pod?

"Fine." She gave a tight nod. "One glass."

"As you wish, m'lady."

"Enough with the 'm'lady' stuff. You're every bit as titled as I am," she huffed, already briskly making her way toward the door, offering a few hip-height goodbye waves to the doctors and nurses newly arrived on shift, all of whom seem to have received some sort of cheesy holiday jumper memo he hadn't caught sight of.

Glowing Rudolph noses? *Bah.* Didn't they know the hazards a battery-powered jumper presented?

"Besides..."

She caught him off-guard by screeching to a halt, eyes blazing with something he couldn't quite identify.

"You earned yours. I didn't."

"I don't know," Matthew countered, appreciating that he was treading on thin ice. "You certainly take it for the team here in the A&E. Didn't I see you dive in front of a nurse today, so she wouldn't get vomited on?"

"Pfft." Amanda shrugged. "I was wearing a disposable gown. She wasn't."

"*And* you've been pulling longer shifts than Dr. Menzies has scheduled."

"That's hardly the stuff of champions, Matthew. And if tacking on a few extra hours to help out in an A&E unit that sorely needs better staffing is the criterion for being titled, then every single staffer in this hospital should be bending a knee before the Queen when she hands out her New Year's honors!"

She swept an arm from one end of the A&E to the other, in an indignant display of disbelief that such a thing hadn't come to pass already, and just as quickly dropped her hands, halfheartedly working them back into the deep pockets of her crimson coat.

Matt nodded. Fair enough. He wasn't going to make her smile. Not today. At least not with idle chatter about who deserved to be a sir or a lady and who didn't. She was right. Sometimes life was simply capricious. And... as in Jenny O'Shea's case...sometimes it was downright cruel.

A hit of cold air promising another frosty night swept across them as they walked out through the automatic hospital doors, past the ambulances on their never-ending cycle of arrivals and departures and out into streets filled to bursting with people hurrying toward home, or a party, or to late-night shopping on Oxford Street—which seemed to be just about every night now that Christmas was less than a fortnight away.

A few minutes of brisk, decidedly silent walking later Amanda whirled round, tears streaming down her face, grief creasing her brow as the day's full weight finally hit her.

"Oh, it's just not *fair*, is it?"

Without a moment's hesitation Matthew pulled her into his arms and held her tight. He couldn't provide words of comfort. There weren't any in this sort of case. No answers. No good reasons. Just life slinging out its challenges one by one while everyone tried to stay afloat.

As he held Amanda close to him he wondered if this was just a bad day taking its toll, or if her response was more personal.

He pulled her in tighter, putting a protective hand across the back of her head as a man haphazardly shouldered a Christmas tree and zigzagged his way to a nearby block of flats. He was hyper-aware of Amanda's jagged breaths against his chest as she fought for control over her emotions.

When a window in the foot traffic cleared he worked them toward a quieter lane, less full of traffic than the main road, and pulled her back close to him, whispering nonsense, really. All he wanted her to know was that she could feel safe in his arms. Safe to cry, to scream, to wail—to pummel his chest if she needed.

As her sobs lessened he put one of his hands to her cheek, brushing his thumb along her jawline until he reached her temple. There, he began to stroke his fingers through the silky blond waves of hair that had fallen out of her loose bun, and it struck him that nothing in his life felt more natural than holding Amanda in his arms. Feeling her fingers tighten in their clutching of his jumper, her heart hammering so fast it beat against his own ribs, her hair brushing underneath his chin as she moaned a long stream of, "No, no, no—it's just not right…"

He agreed. It *wasn't* right. But if you had someone by your side to help carry the load…

You're not that man.

He cleared his throat and used his free hand to dig into his pocket. He pulled out a fresh handkerchief and tucked it into the hand she had pressed against his chest, with a murmur to say that it was clean and he didn't need it back.

When Amanda eventually pulled away, ducking beneath her free-range locks, her expression was almost shy. If she was anything like him—and Matthew had one hell of a feeling she was—doing this—weeping unabashedly—was more intimate for her than the night they'd shared all those years ago.

Again he raised his thumb, swept a couple of lingering tears from her flushed cheeks.

The moment shifted from tender to sensual in an instant.

How she could look so beautiful after sobbing her heart out, he didn't know. Perhaps the honesty of emotion was more powerful than any amount of mascara or eye shadow, or whatever it was she wore to mask her natural beauty. In a league of her own, she was. Stunning.

Unexpectedly she giggled. "Well, that was a bit mortifying."

She pulled away from him, her shoulders wriggling beneath the heavy wool of her winter coat, and looked around her as if suddenly seeing the small cobbled street she must have walked along a thousand times in a brand-new light.

Her expression sobered, and the next time their eyes met the emotion in them was so deep his heart lodged in his throat.

"This is so ironic," she said, shaking her head, breaking their eye contact. "Crying. With *you*. Of all people."

"What do you mean 'of all people'?"

Amanda gave him a sharp look, and her lips were parting to speak when, as if she'd clicked a remote control, he could see the Ice Queen slide back into place.

"Nothing. Apologies. Just being ridiculous, really, aren't I? Though I'm clearly not—it was a tough day. And, seeing as we're going for the same job, it's just… funny."

The job? This wasn't about the *job*.

"It's not exactly laugh-a-minute kind of funny, is it?" Matthew knew she hadn't even come close to explaining herself. What secret was she hiding? "You still up for that glass of wine?"

Again she gave him a curious look. One part disbelief to one part who-are-you-*really*? It was disconcerting. More so to realize he was prepared to tell her. To lay out the hits of history that had turned him into the unsettled, trying-to-do-the-best-he-could-without-getting-hurt man who was standing in front of her.

"Maybe another time?"

He said it before she could. It was written all over her face. She wanted to go home. Alone.

"I'll walk you to your door."

"What? The big strong Knight making sure the poor maiden doesn't crumble to bits the second he's out of view?"

He knew she was teasing, but she'd pretty much hit the nail on the head. He hadn't been able to offer her any comfort. The least he could do was see her safely home.

"Something like that." He matched her teasing tone, before lowering it an octave. "Besides... Who would I have to play with at work if you took to your bed?"

The atmosphere between them thickened.

Everything was going Tilt-A-Whirl, as if he and Amanda were testing one another at each stop on the emotional spectrum. From tears, to polite chitchat, to sudden hits of barely checked desire.

Playfulness twinkled in Amanda's eyes as the tip of her pink tongue nipped out and swept along her full lower lip. "Now, *what* would have you thinking of me in my bed, Dr. Chase?"

A shot of heat blasted his chest apart and swept straight past his belt to parts of his body he was unsuccessfully willing into submission.

Grateful for the protective cover of his overcoat, he fell back a step or two as she pressed the code into the garden square he presumed was across from her house, taking the opportunity to rake the length of her visually.

He knew damn well why his body had taken a trip to

the tropics. He wanted her. Had from the moment he'd laid eyes on her all that time ago—just the same as he did now. Another shockwave of erotic desire taunted him with an image of pressing Amanda up against one of the enormous oaks in the center of the garden and having his wicked way with her. The cool, wintry air would be a titillating contrast to the heat they would create as they moved together in synchronized—

"Do you like the decorations?" she asked, turning back with an innocent expression.

Grateful for the darkness, he murmured something nondescript, stopping himself from reaching out to grab her hand, or drape a protective arm across her shoulders as if they'd been a couple from the beginning of time. That was how natural it felt to be with her. How much he wanted to touch her.

Was it him, or were those sidelong glances she kept giving him sending the same message?

I want you.

A handful of footsteps away from the gate leading out of the garden he went with his gut and pulled her to him, lips lowering without a moment's hesitation until he was kissing her with a near insatiable hunger.

She tasted of lip gloss and salty tears and a natural sweetness he knew belonged just to her. He could hear her murmur his name against his lips, press her hands to his chest, but he persisted. His tongue teased at her lips as he tugged her closer to him, wanting her to feel the effect she was having on him. He groaned when she finally responded, her mouth opening to allow his tongue in, tasting and exploring with the same heated desire he felt. He drew a sharp breath in as she raked her fingers through his hair, making him long for the sensation of her nails scraping along his bare back.

As quickly as the heat of their kisses soared, a frigid wind blew between them and Amanda pushed back, shaking her head, pressing the back of her hand to her lips. Whether she was trying to hold in the sensation of their kisses or to wipe it away was impossible to tell. Her breath was shaky. Cheeks pink again, but for an entirely different reason.

Once more she started shaking her head. "No. No, I can't do this. Not now. Not with—" She bit down hard on her lip and winced.

"Not with what? The job?" He lifted his hands out to his sides. "It's yours if you want it. I can find somewhere else. Do something else."

Her mouth widened in disbelief. "You don't mean that."

She tugged her collar tightly round that telltale pulse-point in her throat. What he wouldn't give to dip down and kiss her right there…

He forced himself to look her in the eye, only to see that her attention was already fully focused on a house opposite the garden gate. A woman was visible in the window, holding up a small boy. Both of them were peering into the square—he presumed to see if Mummy was coming home.

Everything that had been lava-hot in him turned to ice. Family. Responsibility. The two things he wasn't programmed for.

"You're right. I don't." He kept his tone as light as possible, nodding toward the house as he did. "Looks like you'd better get home now. See you tomorrow."

Amanda gave him a distracted look as she raised her

hand to the woman and waved, though they were too far away for them to see her.

He turned to go. He didn't need a reminder that he would never relive those intimately sensual moments with Amanda. Not that he deserved it. Not with his track record.

"Matthew, I—"

He turned back, surprised at the lift of hope in his chest.

"Thank you," she said, lifting the handkerchief. "For everything."

He nodded, the disappointment in his chest becoming leaden. "Goodnight."

He turned and strode off in long-legged strides, until eventually he needed to feel the burn in his chest. Grateful he was still wearing his trainers, he kicked up his pace into a run.

The air bit his face as he pushed, strained against wash after wash of emotion, but his thoughts kept looping back to the same place. His heart. He was falling in love. And that was the one thing he'd promised himself he would never do.

Amanda pressed the door shut behind her and fell back against it, her chest heaving with emotion.

"Goodness, darling! You look absolutely puffed." Auntie Florence appeared out of the sitting room, holding a very sleepy-looking Tristan in her arms. "Did you run home?"

Amanda pressed her hand to her chest—as if the silly gesture would contain the thumping of her heart recovering from *those kisses*—and tried her best to smile.

"How could I not? I didn't want to miss my best little boy before he dropped off into the Land of Nod, did I?"

She reached out her arms, her heart filling with peace as her son mimicked the gesture and all but flew into her arms. "Oops. Easy there, my love. We don't want to use Auntie Flo as a launching pad, now, do we?"

Tristan giggled, tracing his fingers along her face. More than ever Amanda was struck by how much her son was turning into a little Matthew. She pulled one of his small hands into her own and play-nibbled along each of his fingers as if she was a hungry monster, which threw him into another gale of laughter.

A sharp ache filled her chest. One she'd never thought she'd feel. She wished Matthew could see his little boy. Enjoy hearing his laugh. Seeing his smile. It was just so impossible to tell how he would respond, and the desire to protect her son from even the tiniest dust mote of rejection was essential. Tristan was the one person she'd vowed never to fail.

"Darlings, look!" Florence had moved to one of the windows beside the large front door. "It's snowing!"

Amanda pulled the door open, tugging a section of her winter coat round Tristan so he could see and touch his first winter snow.

When they were out on the front steps the air held that singular hushed, thrilling expectancy that only a snowfall in London could bring. As if the millions of people held within the city limits were all holding their breath, waiting for a Christmas miracle.

Amanda scanned the square, her index finger running the length of her lips and back again. Only a handful of people were in the square now…most of them hunched against the cold…none of them the six-foot-something, dark-haired, blue-eyed man who had just kissed her as if she were oxygen itself.

As her heart filled with disappointment she knew with sudden clarity exactly what she wanted her Christmas miracle to be…and ached at the impossibility of achieving the dream.

CHAPTER SEVEN

IF AMANDA HAD thought working with Matthew was high-octane a week earlier, one week closer to Christmas they were hitting a whole new level of anything-you-can-do-I can-do-better. Or maybe it was the whole kissing and then running away to hide in her house thing.

There was no doubting the chemistry between them. It fizzled and crackled throughout the long, wearing shifts. An invisible superfood rendering them both turbo-charged.

For every sprain she had, he would have a compound fracture. For every cardiac arrest that came her way, he would have a severe case of pneumonia.

It was as if they had trading cards of Worst and Silliest Patient Files. Not only did they enjoy "out-doctoring" each other, they enjoyed helping one another. It genuinely felt as if once the scrubs were on they were predestined to work with the other. And once they were off…

She blinked away an image of herself doing a strip-tease in a sexy elf costume… Those thoughts were far too naughty to revisit. Most of the time, anyway.

All very confusing. Particularly when memories of That Night and Those Kisses sent surges of adrenaline through her in the form of a brush of fingers as they handed one another instruments, the heat of his hand on the small of her back as he moved past her with yet another patient, a soft wink masking—just for an instant—those incredible blue eyes.

Ugh. Who was she kidding? The nonstop endorphin rush was undoubtedly The Other Elephant in the Room. The whole I-had-your-child-and-he-lives-round-the-corner elephant.

Hours would go by when she was engrossed in her work and then—*bam!* She'd catch a glimpse of Matthew smiling, or cross paths with him in the waiting room, and each time it was like being struck from behind with an anvil, adding to the weight of the huge secret she was carrying in her chest.

If she could just hold it in for a few more weeks, all the angst would be over and done with. One of them would get the job. The other would go on their merry way. They'd ring in the New Year, no hard feelings, and she'd most likely never see him again.

But then she'd think of poor Jenny O'Shea and her terminally ill son. Would she tell her son's father? What was that saying? A burden shared is a burden halved?

She let her head crack down on the wall next to the assignment board. The longer she waited, the more confusing it became.

Should she tell him? When? How? Casual? Serious? A mix of both? Would he be angry? Thrilled? Would he want to marry her and whisk her away for a life of wedded bliss? Did she even want that?

Stupid question. Of course she'd love that. But maybe…maybe not just yet. Because the chances were much higher that he would head for the hills and prove to her what she'd feared all along: she didn't deserve the perfect life. Not after everything she'd done.

She conked her head against the wall again, ignoring

the curious looks of a passing nurse wearing reindeer antlers, and tried to channel the practice session she'd had out loud in the ladies' loo earlier in the day.

"So…remember the other day, when I sobbed into your chest and then looked up into your beautiful blue eyes? There was some kissing and nothing else in the whole world seemed to matter? Well…turns out I had your baby! Two years ago. *Ha!* Yeah. Funny, isn't it?"

That version had to be scrubbed.

Just like the name of her last patient, which she'd just struck off the list. Her third case of prawn cocktail food poisoning this week. Why the dish was a seasonal favorite was beyond her. Buffet dining often meant food poisoning.

Harrumph. Maybe being a doctor carved just a bit too much magic out of the holiday season. She saw mistletoe poisoning where others saw a chance to kiss their lover.

Mmm… Kissing…

Matthew.

She pushed back from the wall and forced herself to look at the assignment board, vividly aware that she was already tuning in to the sound of Matthew's approaching voice as if he were a homing beacon.

She snorted. *As if.*

At least that was what she kept telling herself to justify not telling him he was a father. She wasn't blind. His flirting wasn't solely reserved for her. *Mostly* for her. *Natch.* She did have her pride. But not all—and that was a daily reminder that Matthew Chase was at the opposite spectrum of your typical family man.

She shrugged her shoulders up tight to her ears and jiggled them up and down a few times, trying to shake some sense into herself. *She* was the one acting like a giddy teen. He…he was just doing his job and making it fun.

Amanda forced herself to focus on the board, pressing her hands into her lower back, taking note of all the same ol', same ol' cases with a whole lot of Good Tidings making the usual injuries take on a more festive flair.

Like the allergy to a Christmas tree she'd treated that morning. Just thinking of the red raw skin the poor girl had revealed beneath her bauble snowman jumper made her wince afresh. *Youch!*

"Dr. Wakehurst?"

She turned and smiled at Dr. McBride. He was wearing a seen-better-days jumper that resembled a green elf's costume and looked his usual weary, not entirely cheery self. He had infant twins at home, he'd confided over a quick cup of tea and a gingerbread Santa Claus. Being here in the chaotic A&E was his "downtime."

She'd commiserated. The first few months after she'd had Tristan it had been as if bottles, nappies, laundry and jiggling him first on one hip and then the other until he finally went off to sleep had eaten her days alive, let alone the midnight hours.

Her gaze drifted across to Matthew. He was swiftly carrying a young child toward the swinging doors that led to Triage. A little boy with blond curls, from the looks of things. His parents didn't seem to be with him. Poor chap. Perhaps he'd been at daycare. There was a center just round the corner that had already sent in a sprain and a chipped front tooth today.

She began to refocus her attention on the relentless flow of conversation at the main desk behind her. One voice in particular stood out.

"I don't care how high on the management chain you need to go, I insist you locate Dr. Wakehurst at once!"

"Auntie Florence?"

She whirled around and saw her auntie's face creased

in frustration, blood on her jacket, her eyes dark with…
Wait a minute. She took off at a run, pulling aside curtain after curtain until she found Matthew and her little baby boy.

"I'm sorry—you can't be in here," Matthew was raising a hand, not looking up from his young charge. Tristan had a head wound—bleeding profusely, as most of them did—and was whimpering softly for his mother.

"It's all right, darling," Amanda soothed, ignoring Matthew entirely as she raced to the bedside and stroked her fingers along her little boy's cheek. "Mummy's right here."

Matthew's eyes snapped to hers and she instantly looked away. "This is your son?"

She nodded, taking in the scene as best she could, but her mind was buzzing with the static of emotion and fear.

No, no, no, this wasn't happening! None of it.

Her son covered in blood. Matthew being the attending physician. Him not knowing this was his own flesh and blood he was treating.

A long cut ran from Tristan's eyebrow up to his hairline. It was difficult to tell how deep it was because of the blood. Head wounds always bled heavily, but when it was your own son…

A swell of nausea rose in her throat. There was so much blood!

"Have you called X-Ray?"

She still couldn't look Matthew in the eye. This was not the way she had planned on letting him know he had a son. She still hadn't entirely decided whether or not she was *ever* going to tell him. Making that decision while her little boy lay in front of her bleeding was too much to contemplate. Right now she was a mother. That had to be her priority.

Matthew pressed a roll of gauze to the wound, issuing instructions to a nurse as he did so to get a suture kit and a few other items.

"I've called X-Ray. We need to speak with whoever was with the little chap—"

"My aunt. Auntie Florence," Amanda snapped, her mind reeling. As ridiculous as it seemed, she felt as if he should know these things. These details. This was his son. *Their* son.

"And his name is Tristan."

Matthew looked up at her, a quizzical expression crossing his face. Just as quickly it passed and he assumed a more professional expression. One she could tell he reserved for relatives who were becoming overwrought.

"Are you sure you're all right to be in here, Amanda? I can get one of the nurses to sit with you. Your boy will be in good hands."

Amanda's draw dropped in disbelief, her tongue went dry and every word in her vocabulary just…*whoosh*… disappeared.

Matthew wasn't allowed to treat Tristan any more than she was.

"He's—"

Matthew's bright blue eyes snapped up to meet hers, his impatience growing. "C'mon. It's make your mind up time, Mummy. Are you going to be a brave girl and help your son by holding his hand, or do we need the nice nurse here to take you out and find you a cup of tea while the doctor takes care of everything?"

"I'm not moving."

She heard the words in slow motion, but saw Matthew register them in double-time. She might have been fighting fiercely for the A&E post, but when it came to her son it was Mama Bear all the way.

"Oh! Thank heavens I've found you, Amanda, darling. I'm terrifically sorry. He was in the bath, playing, and I had a bit of a headache, so I just nipped across the hall to my room for some paracetamol and…" Her fingers flew to her mouth to stem a sob. "Oh, darling. I only took my eyes off him for one minute and the next thing I knew…"

"Did he fall on the tiled floor?" Amanda laid her hand on her aunt's arm. She wasn't angry. Of course she wasn't. But every detail was important.

She scrunched her eyes tight as she listened, willing herself not to think of the most painful times of death she'd had to call. Brain injuries were so unpredictable… Again the nausea threatened to overwhelm her.

"Yes, he was reaching for something on the towel rail. His boats, I think. The ones you gave him for his birthday. I can't imagine how he got the cut—perhaps that old ridiculous cast iron soap holder…"

"Has he had his tetanus shot?" Matthew asked, steadily clearing away the blood, replacing the soaked gauze with a fresh round.

Amanda stood, mesmerized, as she watched his long fingers gently swab across Tristan's forehead. The toddler seemed bewitched by Matthew's eyes, was reaching his hands up to him…or perhaps it was just to the shiny swing of his stethoscope.

"Amanda?" Matthew prompted, with another quick glance in her direction. "Tetanus?"

"He's had the first three doses." Amanda tried to picture the paperwork as she absorbed the sight of the large bump she could now see emerging on her son's forehead. "He's not old enough for the booster."

"How old is he?"

Amanda's blood ran cold.

Just concentrate on the facts.

Matthew was asking the question as a doctor, not as a man trying to determine whether or not this was his son.

"He's just turned two," she forced herself to reply.

The little boy whimpered and let out a cry as Matthew replaced yet another round of gauze.

Florence covered her mouth, her eyes filling with tears as she looked at her grandnephew, pale-faced and tearful on the examination table. "Tristan, darling, are you all right?"

Matthew accepted the suture kit from the nurse, then asked her to make a call up to Neurology to see if there was any chance of getting a CT scan.

"CT scan? Why? Are his pupils—?" Amanda shoved her fist against her mouth.

The moment Matthew truly looked into her little boy's eyes he'd know. He would just *have* to know.

Mistaking her distress for maternal concern, Matthew put on a bright "for children" voice, pulling out his pencil light as he did so. "Seeing as we've got one of the knights of the round table here, I'm sure Tristan will be very brave. He's not lost consciousness, and he presents no signs of cerebrospinal fluid or bruising behind either ear. Without the scan we can't completely rule out a subdural bleed, but he isn't complaining from anything other than the superficial wound and what looks to be shaping up to be a rather impressive bump."

Amanda nodded, practically hearing all the explanations in advance. She knew this. She knew all of it. She was a *doctor*, for goodness' sake. But this was her son and he was being cared for—with tenderness and compassion—by the father she'd thought her boy would never know.

Through some miracle of will, she compelled herself to tune back into Matthew's voice.

"As you know, Dr. Wakehurst, all the scans and X-rays are merely precautionary. A course of action I'm sure you would follow if you were in my shoes."

Matthew ducked his head and looked up at her, impatiently awaiting a nod of agreement. But she just stood there, frozen, staring into those sapphire-blue eyes. If Tristan was being treated by anyone other than Matthew…

"Right." Matthew gave his hands a brisk rub. "I'm just going to get some ice on this bump and glue the wound together before we send the pair of you up to X-Ray. We can get a nurse in to help, if you'd rather not be here."

Matthew looked from Amanda to her aunt and back again.

"How about you two ladies go out and find yourselves—?"

"It's you!" Florence stumbled back a step, staring at Matthew as if she was looking at a ghost.

"I'm sorry?" Matthew ruffled his fingers lightly through Tristan's hair and gave him a reassuring pat on the shoulder before pressing himself up to his full height and looking, more intently this time, from Amanda to Florence. "Have we met?"

"You're—" Florence looked at Matthew, then widened her gaze as she turned to Amanda, as if waiting for her to point out the obvious.

"I'm what?" Matthew glanced down at Tristan. "Ladies, I really need to get our little chap here sorted…"

"You've already told him?" Florence's voice was no more than a whisper as her eyes widened in astonishment.

"Told me what?" Matthew's voice was tight now. "Is there anything I need to know in advance of treating the patient?"

"He's not 'the patient.'" Amanda couldn't hold back any longer. "He's your son."

CHAPTER EIGHT

His *son*?

Everything in Matthew stilled. The symphony music that was the usual soundtrack in the A&E turned into a dull buzzing in his ears. Strangely, he could hear his own heartbeat. The rapid cadence overriding any ability to make sense of what he'd just heard. Beneath his fingertips he could feel the soft silk of the young boy's straw-colored hair. A darker shade of Amanda's more honeyed blond.

Matthew's eyes were glued to Amanda's, willing them to tell a different story, but she returned his gaze with the solid strength of an Amazon princess. Fierce and proud. There wasn't an ounce of apology for having had their son. There was *pride*.

A thousand questions clamored for supremacy, but his ability to comprehend the news demanded only one. A repeat. As if hearing it again would make it real instead of this halfway house between reality and…was it a nightmare or a dream come true?

"What did you say?"

Tears flooded Amanda's eyes, blurring her hazel irises into a wash of unchecked emotion. "He's your son." She blew out a trembling breath. "*Our* son."

She looked away—which was just as well, because

he was fairly certain he wasn't giving an ideal response. There wasn't even the chance to register a pregnancy. There was a living, breathing little boy's future at stake.

Unable to look down at the table, he closed his eyes and systematically went back through the minutes—was it five already?—he'd been with the boy.

Tristan.

He had a *son*.

Focus!

Think.

He'd lifted him from Amanda's aunt's arms when he'd seen the blood. Done a cursory pupil response the moment he'd laid him on the table.

What color were his eyes?

This was his son. Why couldn't he remember the color of his eyes?

He willed the color to come to him. As clear as day he could see his brother. Bright blue eyes—just like his. A shock of wild dark hair. A smattering of freckles he'd always said should have belonged to someone else. A *girl*. One of the many things he'd added to his list of "Things I Hate About Being Charlie." He'd had a list. An actual list. They'd found it when they had finally gathered the strength to clear out his room.

"Matthew, please. Can we get him up to X-Ray?" Amanda pleaded. "If there's any internal bleeding…"

She left the sentence unfinished, her fingers unconsciously templing into the prayer position and coming to a rest against her lips. He saw her lips move again but heard no sound.

Please.

It struck Matthew that he was seeing Amanda in an entirely different light.

The mother of his child.

She was beautiful. Arrestingly so.

Now he understood with vivid clarity why her curves bore the swoop and ripe essence of a woman who'd borne a child. She was fiery. Smart. A talented doctor. A man would count himself more than lucky to have a woman like her by his side. Blessed, even.

And yet it all sang of commitment. Commitment he had vowed never to be a part of.

And then he snapped his mental switch on. The one he always used when his emotions grew too powerful, his memories turned too dark.

"Of course. Would you like to bring him up?"

Amanda nodded, swiping at the tears spilling down her cheeks.

He was seized by an urge to wipe them away. To pull her into a strong half hug as they turned to their son so he could run his fingers through his little boy's hair again and tell them everything would be all right. But he knew more than most that life had a way of careening out of control. He'd promised his parents he would look after his brother that day and—

How could he be trusted to care for a son?

Taking a deep breath, he chose his words carefully. "I think it would be best if I handed this case over to another doctor to oversee. We'll get a nurse in to glue this wound now that the bleeding has ebbed."

"You're not even going to glue the wound?" Amanda's eyes widened in disbelief.

"No, I—"

He blinkered his vision, focusing solely on the wound. His instruments. Completely unable to look his son in the face. He just couldn't.

He gave Amanda a curt nod, then pulled back the

curtain. "I'll just pop out to find a nurse and let Dr. Mc-Bride know you'll be off the roster. Won't be a minute."

He pulled the curtain back into place, leaving an open-mouthed Amanda behind it, and took a step forward—willing, praying for the wash of emotion threatening to engulf him to stay at bay.

This was ridiculous. He was a grown man. He couldn't respond to the news that he was a father with fear. Just run away. He'd been in war zones, for heaven's sake.

By choice, he swiftly reminded himself. When his parents had made it more than clear that the Chase Family was no longer a family he'd gone off and found his own way. First at med school. Then in the army. But always with a protective shield curved around his heart.

He tipped his head up, surprised to note he was almost smiling. He could just hear Dr. Menzies's voice: "Taking on a job like this means no more bunking off to foreign climes, my boy. There's no running away from your demons here. There's only overcoming them."

It looked as if life had thrown him the full package. Fear of commitment. Fear of responsibility. Fear of... He shook his head as the word he knew terrified him the most popped into his head.

Love.

After losing his brother—a big brother he had adored as if he were Hercules himself—then growing up in the shadow of his parents' unstemmable grief, Matthew knew more than anything that he was not capable of that sort of deep, unconditional, selfless love. And a child deserved a father's entire heart.

In a few swift strides he was at the central assignment desk. He briskly organized for a nurse to see Tristan and to direct Amanda up to X-Ray. Ignoring the raised eyebrows, he asked Dr. McBride for the case to be referred to another doctor and that he be assigned only to all the significant trauma cases that regularly swept through their doors. "Research," he called it.

Avoidance, more like.

He knew he was pulling rank, but to be honest that was the only thing he had right now. The power to say yes and no. And there was no way he was publicly re-cusing himself from someone's medical treatment before he had a chance to process the fact that the child was his own flesh and blood.

He heard the crackle of a paramedic team radio com-ing through. They had just picked up a cyclist who had been hit by a lorry blindly swinging round a corner. He would never wish anyone harm, but by God he was re-lieved to have an anonymous patient to pour his ener-gies into.

Someone he could actually help.

An hour later, after the cyclist had been sent into sur-gery, Matthew devoted himself to every serious case he could get his hands on. One successfully resuscitated cardiac arrest later Matthew couldn't take it anymore. There weren't enough compound fractures or subdural hematomas to keep his mind off the overwhelming fact that his life had just changed forever.

He was a father.

Finally accepting that a twelve-hour shift, a twenty-four-hour shift or even working until he dropped from exhaustion wouldn't change things, Matthew did the only thing he could to try and process what Amanda had told him about her little boy. *Their* little boy.

Five minutes later he was standing in Maternity with a day-old baby boy in his arms, doing his best to ignore the sidelong glances the green and red scrub-clad nurses were shooting his way.

Tough.

He'd missed this part. Missed those vital moments of connection a father had with a child when it first entered into the world. He was surprised to feel the sting of loss. He hadn't been there.

It was so easy to imagine being there for Amanda. Encouraging her throughout her labor, feeling her fingers digging into his hand, doing her best to cut off his circulation when the pain overwhelmed her. Him calling her a wimp but gently pressing a soft, cool cloth to her forehead, wiping away the beads of sweat that labor inevitably produced, all the while looking into her warm hazel eyes in sheer wonder at what the two of them had created together.

Not that he'd been invited.

It was a blunt reminder that, all things considered, Amanda hadn't exactly rolled out the welcome carpet. They'd been working together for almost three weeks now and she hadn't said a word. He could hardly blame her.

While the baby in his arms was perfectly adorable—tiny fingers doing their best to wrap round his index finger, little mouth shaping into Os and smiles when he tickled the little tyke's tummy—Matthew was vividly aware that his heart wasn't beating any faster, his pupils weren't dilating, and the surge of intense pride and disbelief he'd felt when he'd looked into Tristan's clear blue eyes…dead ringers for his own…it wasn't there.

But he owed Amanda support. Financial. Emotional.

He shook his head.

The financial support wasn't a problem. But the emotional part…? He wasn't the guy for that sort of thing.

He could provide a shoulder to cry on, at least…on the rare occasions she let herself cry. And time, he supposed. Every single mother he'd ever met wished for a thirty-eight-hour day.

He gently placed the infant back in its little tray bed and that was when it struck him—a feeling so sharp it was as if he'd been slashed in two. He stared at his empty hands feeling an intense, gut-wrenching loss at no longer holding a child close to him. Feeling its weight, its utter dependency upon him.

And it scared him to the bone.

"He's been a very brave little boy. Haven't you, Tristan?" The X-ray technician rubbed a hand along Tristan's shoulder and, in the true style of a toddler dealing with a myriad of "new," Tristan curled into his mother's shoulder for a cuddle, arms wrapped tightly around her neck.

Amanda gave the technician an apologetic smile. "He's obviously not at his most gregarious today."

He'd been fine with Matthew.

But Matthew's not here.

Amanda crammed that thought into her mind's No Go cupboard and forced herself to focus. This was precisely what she'd thought would happen if she'd told him when she had found out she was pregnant: not interested.

"Not to worry." The technician smiled. "I don't blame him. That is one impressive bump!" He grinned, then fixed Amanda with a solid gaze. "I suspect you know this already, seeing as…" He waved his hand the length of her scrubs and white coat. "But I wouldn't be doing my job if I didn't remind you of the concussion checklist once you've got the little guy home."

"Auntie Florence?"

Amanda called along the corridor to her aunt, who

had spent the last three hours intently examining the hospital's art display.

"Would you like to come and hear what we need to look out for, just in case Tristan presents with any other symptoms?"

"Oh, no, dear. You go on ahead." Her aunt shook her head and fastidiously returned to inspecting the enormous mural in front of her.

Curious. Usually Florence was really hands-on. Amanda tried to shrug it off, but the repeated niggling that had driven her to apply for this job returned. It wasn't fair to rely on her aunt for so much childcare. Whether or not she got the job, Amanda knew in her heart it was time to look into hiring a nanny sooner rather than later. Even if it did stretch her income to the outer limits.

She suggested that her aunt head home and said they would meet her there in a few minutes. She'd make some pasta once Tristan had gone to sleep.

As she watched her walk toward the lift Amanda's heart ached for her. It wasn't her fault. Toddlers were every bit as off balance as she felt now. And Tristan had been lucky.

A nanny. A nanny would help.

She hoped her thoughts would ease the strain on Florence's hunched shoulders as she disappeared into the lift—no doubt to go and check if the heating in their old home was working today.

Amanda huffed out a quick laugh as she turned back to the X-ray technician. If only nannies hung from Christmas trees as abundantly as decorations. Not that she'd gotten round to decorating yet.

It was just another one of life's trials to overcome. She'd start hunting for someone to help tonight. Even if it meant no new clothes for the next year. That was a sacrifice she'd be more than happy to make. There wasn't a chance in the universe she'd go crawling to her parents, let alone Matthew for a hand-out. Not a chance in hell, either.

Amanda fixed on a smile and nodded at the X-ray technician to go ahead.

"As you know, we didn't see anything, but sometimes these injuries are tricky and complications can rear up later."

He rattled through the list Amanda had already been running in her head on a loop as she'd watched her little boy lying so still in the CT machine and then on the X-ray table.

Vomiting clear fluid, blood, blurry or double vision, slurred speech, pupils of unequal size, seizures…

The list went on and on and finally she had to stop the technician. She knew the signs. She knew the symptoms. She just prayed she wasn't going to see any of them in her son.

"I think we're good. Probably the best thing to do will be to get this little guy home for—" She flicked her eyes up to the wall clock. "Goodness! It's well past seven o'clock. You should be in bed, my little poppet!"

She nuzzled against his golden curls, which were turning ever darker as he grew older. More reminders of Matthew were still to come. Of that she had no doubt. But Tristan wasn't Matthew. He was her little boy.

She popped a soft kiss on his cheek and protectively pulled her doctor's coat around him. The gesture shot her back to the days when he had still been an infant in swaddling. When she'd never felt more love in her heart and less prepared for the journey she'd been about to embark on. Today she felt the same off balance sensation about her future. Knowing Matthew wanted nothing to do with his little boy was…

She'd known it somewhere deep in her heart already, but marrying that with reality… She was sucking a lot of lemons today. And it wasn't even close to lemon season.

"C'mon, Tris," she whispered into his ear. "Let's get you home and into bed."

A few moments later Amanda had grabbed her things from her locker and told her son they were almost home. Bed for him. Pasta and then bed for her. Not having to think about anything for a few hours would be a blessing.

With Tristan half asleep on her shoulder, she exited the changing room—only to come face to face with Matthew. He didn't speak for a moment. He looked at the pair of them with such intensity it was as if he was trying to memorize what they looked like…as if this would be the last time he laid eyes on them.

"We're just off home." Amanda finally broke the silence, taking a small step forward so that Matthew would take the hint and step aside. No such luck.

"Here," he said, his voice rough with emotion. "He looks like quite a load. Let me."

She watched as he awkwardly extended his hands toward her, astonished to discover that every cell in her body wasn't screaming, *No, no, no!* She caught her breath in disbelief. And then a wash of *He's mine!* hit her every bit as hard as if she'd been hit by an actual car.

"Oh. Gosh." Amanda's eyes were moving everywhere but towards the vicinity of Matthew as she hugged Tristan closer to her. "That's awfully generous of you, Dr. Chase, but you've had a long day and—"

Matthew put up a hand to stop her spluttering.

"Easy now, tiger. First of all, it's still Matthew. I think we've gone well past the formal stage in this…" He'd been about to say *this affair*, but bit off the word and started again. "This is an offer to carry your son home... let's take things at face value, shall we?"

Matt was trying to sound good-natured, but even after the short time she'd known him she could tell the gesture was taking a Herculean effort.

Your son.

Not *our* son.

She hid the sting of his word-choice by tipping her head toward her son's curls and inhaling the distinct little boy scent. Soap, Marmite sandwiches and growth.

This wasn't what she wanted. And it was why she'd hoped never to run into Matthew again. Having Matthew in their lives would only complicate things. Which was exactly why the moment she'd seen that telltale plus sign on the pregnancy test she'd vowed never to let him know.

Her parents had made it more than clear what a burden she'd been to them. The last thing she was going to do was bring a child into the world and expose him to someone who would think the same.

"C'mon." Matthew gave her a soft smile as she shifted the dead weight of her now sleeping son from one shoulder to the other. "Hand him over. Trust me..." he put on a barmy grin "... I'm a doctor."

If her arm hadn't been cramping for the past twenty minutes she would have said no. But that was just an excuse. Matthew had every right to hold his son. Every right to offer help and not be turned away. She owed him explanations. She owed him a debt of gratitude for unwittingly giving her a son.

She blinked up at him, a note of wariness in her voice as she made her decision. "You're sure?"

There wasn't a thing about Matthew that looked certain, but he was still holding out his hands, waiting to accept the weight of their sleeping son in his arms.

As their arms crossed and brushed against each other's Amanda was struck by such a strong sensation of déjà vu it was as though Father Time himself had taken this moment and set it aside just for the pair of them.

Their gazes clashed against each other as Amanda pulled her hands back and let Matthew take the full weight of their child. She'd expected to feel a core-deep sensation of loss when her arms, now empty, fell to her sides. Instead, seeing Matthew gently cupping their son's head in his large, capable hands, she experienced a warm buzz of security she hadn't felt in a long time. Maybe not ever.

"Right, then." Matthew's expression turned all business. "Let's get this little man home and I'll be one my way!"

CHAPTER NINE

MATTHEW WASN'T BLIND.

The tiniest of winces betrayed Amanda's response to his clumsy attempt to make this incredibly awkward scenario a bit lighter.

No.

"Awkward" wasn't really the best word to describe finding out mid-shift—mid-*patient*—from the woman he was trying to stop himself from falling head over heels in love with that said patient was in fact his own flesh and blood.

Blindsided. Overwhelmed. Speechless.

Those would do for starters.

Matthew had thought he'd experienced a full gamut of emotions the day his brother died. Excitement for the holidays. Joy that his brother was home from yet another harrowing tour. Bone-aching grief when his brother's "quick trip to the attic" had been his last.

What a fool. All Matthew had done that day was begin a lifetime of embodying the darker spectrum of his emotional world—completely turning himself off to the glowing rainbow, the *lightness* a man could experience when he found out he was a father.

He had a child.

A son.

One he was now holding in his arms.

No matter how vehemently he had vowed never to have a child of his own, never to bear the responsibility for someone else's life, the elation was impossible to fight. As if it was programmed into him the same way every living soul needed water and food to survive.

Light shadows were darkening under Amanda's eyes and she was unable to mask her wary expression as she watched him holding their child. Worry did that to a person. And a heavy workload. He could barely manage his own time, let alone imagine juggling a full-time job and parenting.

But Amanda had done this on her own for two years, so he could handle a ten-minute walk in the snow.

As Tristan wriggled amidst the folds of his mother's medical coat, to snuggle closer into his chest, he was shaken at just how precious a bond it was to have this small, innocent child...naive and full of trust...instinctually believing he was one of the good ones. Someone to trust.

Tristan's hand reached out, then curled gently round his neck as Matthew wrapped an arm around him, vividly aware of his son's simple faith that this stranger who was holding him, caring for him, would do his very best never to let any harm come to him. He knew in his heart this was true. For every day he had on earth he would care for and protect Tristan and Amanda with every ounce of fight and drive he had in him.

"Right!" Amanda pressed her fingers to her lips for a moment, clearly processing the sight of father and son together. "It's still snowing out there—shall we get a move on?"

A few staffers called out to them as they left, with wishes of good health for Tristan, rest for Amanda. There were a handful of curious looks thrown in Matthew's direction. Had they been strangers at Bankside they would have looked like any other couple worried about their son, intent on bringing him to the family home.

"Look at all the lights Tris…" Amanda was a step behind Matthew, eagle-eyeing her son as they worked their way to the crossing at the far end of the hospital.

Matthew's eyes followed her finger as she pointed out the brilliantly lit baubles and snowflakes, all blurring a little behind the gently falling snow. For anyone else it would have been magical. For Matthew it was like walking through the sands of time to that day so long ago, when he'd told his parents he would be fine keeping an eye on his brother while they went out Christmas shopping.

If only he hadn't been sidetracked by those ridiculous video games Charlie had brought him. It was why he'd never played one since. The same reason he gave the bulk of the profits from his family's company to charity. What good was sitting in a mansion with all of the trappings knowing you didn't have the ability to look after someone you loved?

"We just want to take a left round this corner, although it *is* possible to cut through the alley." Amanda pointed her gloved hand across the web of streets as if she were an air stewardess, pointing out emergency exits.

"Let's play it safe and skip the alley, shall we?"

No answer.

He suspected her detailed directions to a place he'd already been were from a nervous mind trying to fill the silence. Or a test. This sort of thing was precisely why he'd volunteered to help bring Tristan home. To make things clear. Establish boundaries. Make…*rules*. He didn't do guessing or games or anything that involved grey areas.

A one-night stand. That was all it had been meant to be. Never mind the fact he'd thought of Amanda near enough every day since then. A woman that exemplary… He glanced across at her, saw her delicate features concentrating on the road they were crossing. You didn't forget a woman of this caliber.

It made saying no to other women a breeze. He asked himself one simple question each time a conversation turned into a flirtation.

Does she meet The Amanda Standard?

For every single one of them the answer was no.

That didn't mean he was ready to settle down and get married with a pre-made family, though.

Matthew cleared his throat, the choke of building emotion overtaking his fundamental desire to keep things as businesslike as he could. "I suppose we'd better have a talk."

Amanda kept her gaze straight ahead, her footsteps crisply clicking heel-toe, heel-toe across the pavement. "I told my aunt I'd make some pasta once I got Tristan to bed. Perhaps you'd like to join us?"

He'd been hoping to speak to her alone, but having a referee was probably a good idea. Even if Auntie Florence would be entirely biased toward her niece and great-nephew. As she should be.

Family.

It had been so long since he'd been in anything resembling a family. He had an uncle somewhere out there. And cousins. But in the wake of Charlie's death his parents had been intent on drowning their sorrows in booze and affairs, and everyone who'd tried their best to help— family, friends—had eventually drifted off to live their own lives.

"Pasta would be nice," Matthew said, before quickly adding, "As long as I'm not intruding."

Amanda gave him a sidelong glance. One that spoke volumes. Of *course* he was intruding. She would have told him about her pregnancy two years and nine months ago if she'd wanted him involved in their lives.

Their intentions had seemed so clear back then. Two people interested in one night of disappearing into each other. And disappear they had. He didn't know what pain or dark thoughts she'd been trying to escape that night, and he certainly hadn't pulled out the My Brother Killed Himself on My Watch card.

But that was then, and single mother Amanda was a very different type of Cinderella now.

She had hardly been able to disguise her horror when he'd appeared outside the doctors' lounge. It must have taken an enormous leap of faith to hand over her son to him. For that was who he was. *Her* son. He would offer to help support Tristan. Of course. It was the least he could do. Especially with Amanda blithely mentioning chilblains.

He made a note to make a few calls about installing central heating into the house. He wouldn't have his son and the mother of his child suffering from the cold.

"And just across the square here."

"I've been in the square before, Amanda."

We kissed the daylights out of each other. Remember?

"Mmm…" Amanda pushed the gate open without so much as a sideways look at the large Douglas Fir wrapped in a swirl of fairy lights. It was even kitted out with enormous weatherproof "presents" he hadn't noticed the other day.

Presents. If only he hadn't pleaded with his parents

for that special gaming device. They'd had to queue for hours.

Would've. Should've. Could've.

These were things the world was built on.

Done. Over. Move on.

That was reality.

"Are you coming?"

Amanda held the gate open and waited until he was well past her before circling back round and shutting the gate. Still no eye contact. No mention of the obvious physical attraction they had for one another. Or the son he was carrying in his arms.

"You won't catch anything contagious, you know." Matthew tried to give her a good-natured elbow in the ribs, but missed as she briskly walked past him.

"Sorry?" She reeled on him. "What's that meant to mean?"

"If you look at me. I haven't changed from the last time you saw me. I just—"

He stopped, slipping his arm protectively up his son's small back, acutely aware of the toddler's hand splayed out on his chest, warming the spot directly above his heart. Five perfect little boy fingers.

"This is a lot to process. I should've come with you to X-Ray, but—"

"You're not the *only* one processing," she fired back at him in a shout-whisper, hackles raised, emotions freed, as if being a few hundred meters from the hospital had finally unlocked a cupboard full of simmering emotion.

Matt reached out to touch her arm and she batted it away.

"Don't. Please. I just—"

Amanda stopped, her fingers covering her mouth as she muttered a few words he couldn't quite catch. Something close to "the last thing in the universe" she'd been hoping for, if his bat-like hearing was fine-tuned enough.

She crossed her arms over her chest and huffed out a sigh. "Let's just…let's just go in and get this over with. I'll withdraw my candidacy for the job in the morning and then you won't have to worry about seeing us ever again."

"Hey! Hang on a minute. A few hours ago I didn't know I had a two-year-old son. Now that I do…"

My whole life has taken a turn I'd never imagined.

"Just give me some time to get used to the idea. We don't know what direction this is going to take—"

"We?" Amanda cut him off with a disbelieving shout, then regrouped into a low growl when Tristan stirred. *"We* are not a 'we.' Tristan and I—*that's* a we. Tristan and you…? Not so much."

Something deeply instinctive roiled in Matthew's chest. Or was it a new part of his heart awakening to the inexplicable pride and love that came from being a parent? He didn't know.

He was the last person his parents had been interested in after his brother had died. His father had found comfort in work and whiskey. His mother had not even bothered to disguise the fact that she was having affairs, finally moving halfway across the world to erase the past she no longer wanted to acknowledge. He hadn't heard from her in years. For all he knew she was still on the go. Still seeking peace.

Amanda's barely contained frustration was threatening to bleed across to him.

The lyrics of the song the hospital choir had been singing popped into his head—"Let there be peace on earth…"

He finished it in a whisper. "And let it begin with me."

He gestured for Amanda to carry on walking, resisting the urge to ruffle the snowflakes from her hair, "C'mon. This is new terrain for both of us. We may as well get in the warm and get Tristan to sleep. Agreed?"

Amanda glared at him, hands on hips. She was looking fit to snatch her son right out of his arms, and in truth he didn't blame her. He was still reeling. For the first time in his life he was genuinely up in the air about having a family of his own.

For the last fifteen years the answer had always been a solid *no*.

And now, with a woman he was centimeters away from being in love with, feeling the weight of his little boy in his arms, with his little hands and his toddler scent and eyes that felt like looking into a mirror, everything had changed.

There was, of course, the vital task of trying to establish a relationship with the woman who looked prepared to scratch his eyes out if so much as a single hair on her son's head was hurt. Not a single thing about the situation screamed *easy*. But he knew in his heart he damn well wasn't going to let Amanda call all the shots. Half the reason this little boy existed was because of *him*. And the other half was because Amanda had found him every bit as desirable as he'd found her.

They worked together and played together as if they had been made for one another. Now they were going to have to find a way to build on that. Parent together.

"Well, get a move on, if you're coming," Amanda snapped. "It's the one over there with the wreath."

Matt looked across the square, following the line her finger hand drawn to the black and white bricked doorway arches where he'd seen… Ah, it must have been Auntie Florence and Tristan in the window. And…yes.

There she was again. Anxiously peering out into the darkness, waiting for them to come home.

"Right. then. Let's get you both home."

"Do you want to see him being tucked into bed?"

Amanda was unwrapping her scarf, barely resisting the urge to flick it at Matthew who, to his credit, was simply standing in the entryway, patiently holding her son—*their son*—and waiting for her to regain some semblance of maturity.

Matthew shook his head in the negative.

"Oh? Too close for comfort? Too much like parenting?"

Matthew's expression hardened, his eyes crackling with barely suppressed anger. "You don't know a thing about me, so watch what you say."

"As if any woman could get to know a thing about you, with all your smooth lines and back-off-I-don't-do-intimacy vibes. Well, don't think you need to stick around on my account. Go on, then. You know where the door is."

She flicked her hands at him as if shooing an enormous chicken out of her entryway.

"Off you go."

She yanked off her coat so aggressively the sleeves turned inside out, then practically threw it at the wooden coat-stand in the entryway. Matthew reached out to steady it as her heavy coat set the antique stand swaying but she was on a roll.

"I suppose you're too busy lining up the girls for your next conquest to stick around long enough for a bedtime story for your son."

"Is that what you think you were?" Matthew ground out, covering his son's head with a protective hand. "A conquest?" The disdain in his eyes was almost palpable.

"It doesn't matter what I think—it matters what *you* think, and I don't remember my phone ringing off the hook."

"I don't remember a certain Cinderella sticking around long enough for me to ask for her number, let alone her name." He arced a brow at her, daring her to contest him.

Amanda reached out to take Tristan from Matthew, her head spinning with too many thoughts. Even the softness of her son's body in her arms wasn't enough to stop her thoughts twisting and turning. Why were they fighting? Matthew was obviously trying to do the right thing. The mature thing. And all she wanted to do was battle this intense surge of longing she felt for them to be a family in the only way she knew…by pushing him away.

"Well, a girl has her—"

She stopped herself. She had been about to say "standards," but Matthew ticked every box in her head, heart, and—she had to face it—her erogenous zones. He was perfect, and she didn't deserve perfect. And she certainly wasn't going to corner him into doing something he didn't want to do.

"A girl has her what?" Matthew pressed. "Pride? Dignity? Secrets?"

She nestled her face into her son's curls, trying to collect her thoughts and stop the threatening sting of tears.

Matthew had hit the nail on the head with all three of his questions. After her ridiculous Las Vegas marriage had ended so cruelly she'd kept everyone at arm's length. Further if possible. And the only reason she was fighting Matthew right now was because she knew she didn't deserve his help.

But the fire she saw in his eyes meant only one thing. He cared. He wanted to be involved. And just the idea of living up to anyone's expectations besides Tristan's scared the living daylights out of her. She'd let her parents down so much. And John. She'd been a girl on a quest for something solid only to discover what she thought had been real had been built on a fiction. And she was terrified to open her heart only to have it thrown back in her face.

"Darling?"

Amanda looked up to the stairwell to see her aunt leaning over the wooden rail, a lace handkerchief pressed to her lips.

"Is everything all right, my love?"

"Yes." Amanda nodded, suddenly feeling exhausted. "Just… Matthew's come along to help."

"He's here?" Florence drew away from the banister and out of sight.

"Yes, he's…" Amanda shot a quick apologetic glance at Matthew. "I'll go up and check she's all right and put Tristan to bed. The kitchen's just through that door there, at the end. Pour yourself a glass of wine, if you can find some, and I'll be down in a minute to fix some supper."

"How about I make supper?" Matthew looked toward the kitchen door before shifting his gaze up toward Florence. "That is, if you and your aunt trust me not to poison you and you're happy for me to make myself at home."

Home.

If only…

Amanda gave him a tight smile of thanks and nodded. "If you don't mind, that would be really helpful. And the kitchen's the warmest room in the house, so it's probably best you stay in there. I think there's pasta in…"

Matthew reached out and gave her shoulder a soft squeeze. Another tenderness she didn't deserve. She strained against the growing sting of tears as he spoke.

"I'll be fine. If you like simple bachelor's fare you're in luck. It's my specialty."

Unable to speak as the swell of gratitude grew in her chest, Amanda nodded and swiftly turned away, so he wouldn't see the sheen of tears glazing her eyes form into drops and skid down her cheeks.

"Take your time," she heard Matthew call behind her. "I promise I won't turn into a pumpkin."

And I promise I'll try my best not to run away.

CHAPTER TEN

MATTHEW LIFTED THE wooden spoon to his lips and tasted the simple sauce he'd made from the handful of ingredients Amanda had on hand in her larder. A tin of tomatoes. A few slices of bacon. An onion that looked as if it had seen its peak a couple of days earlier.

The army had taught him to improvise, so he was pleased. There was a smattering of other food, suitable for a toddler, but this largesse didn't seem to stretch to providing for the adults in the house.

He looked up at the ceiling when he heard a long scraping noise. Wood against wood. His gut reaction was to go and help, but something told him Amanda needed time alone with her son. If she needed him he would let him know.

He almost laughed at the thought. If the last two years were anything to go by, waiting for Amanda to ask him for help would be like waiting for pigs to fly.

He pulled the freezer door open, hoping to find just a little something extra to add to the sauce. It was completely empty save the remains of a bag of peas. This was ridiculous! Thank goodness he knew Tristan had eaten at the hospital, otherwise—

Otherwise nothing.

He gave himself a sharp mental slap. Amanda was

working full-time. Her aunt was elderly and seemed to be the only one looking after the child—Tristan—all day. It obviously didn't leave much time for shopping, and it was hardly as if the boy looked malnourished. This was obviously just an off-day in the groceries department.

Even so, he began adding to the list of things he wanted to put right—including a regular home delivery of staples.

He might not be offering her his heart, but he could certainly fill up her bare cupboards.

He turned at the sound of the swinging door behind him that must have been the servants' entrance in the house's glory days. Amanda slipped into the kitchen, a tartan blanket wrapped round her shoulders, all the while rubbing her hands together and blowing on them.

"Everything all right upstairs?" Matthew asked.

"Yes. Tristan's gone straight to sleep, as expected, and Auntie Florence has insisted on staying with him for a while. The 'first watch' she called it. She made me drag one of her chaise longues in beside his bed."

"*One* of them?"

"Yes." Amanda gave a wry smile. "It's her thing. We've got about five littered about the place."

"No supper for her?"

Amanda shook her head. "She seems pretty upset about Tristan. I've been meaning to get a nanny for a while now. I was just waiting on—" She stopped and gave her feet a little stomp, as if knocking snow off them.

"Waiting on getting a full-time job?" Matthew guessed.

That wasn't good. He didn't want to take money away from Amanda if she needed it. Sure, he wanted the job, but at the expense of their welfare? *No.* That didn't sit right. None of it sat right. Her family was one of the wealthiest in London, if the newspapers' "Rich List" was anything to go by. Weren't her parents helping her at *all*?

Trying to connect the dots, he watched Amanda make the decision not to respond, deflecting his question by making a show of walking into the kitchen and tugging the blanket more snugly round her shoulders.

"Brr! You can see your breath upstairs—" She glanced up at him, then quickly continued, her voice defensive. "Tristan's room has got a space heater in it. He's fine."

Matthew raised his hands, still holding the spoon. "I'm not here to judge—just to…stir the pot."

"Yeah, you've stirred things up, all right." Amanda glowered.

Something in Matthew snapped. He'd been trying his best to be grown up about this, but if she wasn't going to play along… *No dice.*

"If I'm not mistaken, I believe *I'm* the one who just found out he has a toddler. You've had just a bit longer to get used to the idea. And more than enough time to decide I wasn't worth telling."

"That's not fair. That's not why I didn't tell you!" Amanda protested.

"Oh, no? Well, what was it, then? It certainly wasn't lack of opportunity. It's not like we haven't been working twelve-hour days together, is it? Or that the flames of desire have been tamped. I felt the heat in your kisses the other night, so don't you dare tell me keeping my son a secret wasn't a calculated move."

He took in a deep breath in an attempt to slow the rush of emotion charging through his chest—his heart—but he couldn't. This was *his* son, too! Didn't he have a right to know?

"I had to wait for a freak accident to find out I have

a child? Do you have *any* idea how that makes me feel? Knowing I am that low in your estimation?"

Amanda angrily pulled her hair into a ponytail that swung from shoulder to shoulder as she glared at him and then at the ceiling and back again. "It wasn't that. It wasn't *any* of those things. So you can keep your healthy ego intact."

"This isn't about my ego, Amanda. It's about my son. It's about *us*."

He hated the cruel note his voice kept striking, but was incapable of stopping it as a new revelation hit.

"Or is this actually all about *your* ego? Keeping up appearances, is it? I'm not your type? Not blue-blooded enough? Mummy and Daddy wouldn't approve?"

"Stop!" Tears welled in Amanda's eyes. "I've already said. It wasn't any of those things."

As quickly as the rage had flared in Matthew it died away. There was something in Amanda's voice—her entire body language, in fact—that was all but screaming one simple thing. She wanted his help but felt she shouldn't ask for it. Couldn't ask for it for reasons only she knew.

It hurt…but not as much as falling back on his age-old insecurity of not being good enough. *Why* did he feel so powerless to combat that one excruciating fear? He was a soldier. A doctor. A Knight of the British Empire! It was foolish to let himself be hobbled by something that should have been diluted by the passing of time. And yet he was still a teenager in his heart, bearing his pain into adulthood. And from the looks of things Amanda had her own share of troubles that she'd been dragging around.

He slid the spoon back into the sauce and leant against the counter. "How about a deal?"

Amanda tensed and he held up a "wait for it" hand.

"Let's say that for tonight—" He shook his head and corrected himself. "That until *Christmas* you and I cut each other some slack. I'm not saying we're going to be able to sort everything out, but we have to be able to speak about Tristan. Otherwise things at the hospital could get tricky. And if there is one thing I *do* know about you it's that you like to give your best at work."

"You want to talk about him so that we're good at work? *Unbelievable.*"

He narrowed his gaze for a moment. Did she want more? Her taut expression and defensive body stance was hardly the language of love, but perhaps she was as much of a stranger to genuine courtship as he was.

Time to behave as if you're wearing your long trousers now, son.

"I'm trying to say that you don't have to do this alone anymore. How we sort it will take more than one bowl of pasta's worth of discussion, and in the meantime that A&E over there needs our help. I don't think you want to let them down any more than I do." He dipped his head and peered at her, trying to weasel out some form of a smile. "Is it a deal?"

Amanda's shoulders dropped. "I know. I'm sorry. It's just…"

"Just a lot to digest," he finished for her with a soft smile.

He was feeling it, too. Especially as she'd turned up in the kitchen spitting fire and… *Oh, no.* Why had she gone and dropped that blanket on the chair? It was a move designed to fight fire with a whole different variety of fire.

Gone were the work clothes. In their place was a form-fitting onesie that shouldn't be sexy, but on Amanda… mmm… And that bosom-to-belly-button zipper was just calling out to be toyed with. Crikey. He didn't stand a chance.

"Should we shake on it?" Amanda held out her hand and padded across the kitchen tiles, hand extended.

"Are those *unicorn* slippers?"

"Yes," Amanda replied, as smoothly as if he'd asked if they were the latest designer's elite creation. She pointed one of her toes, ballerina-style. "You like?"

"Mmm. Lovely." He gripped the spoon and gave his pasta sauce a stir, knowing he'd far rather be unzipping her outfit and showing her just how much he liked everything about her.

"I thought we were going to shake on it?" Amanda extended her hand, her body giving a little shimmy beneath that shouldn't-be-sexy-but-was ensemble of hers.

"I'm good with a verbal agreement."

Matthew developed a fastidious interest in micromanaging the stirring of the sauce, vividly aware of Amanda dropping her hand, crossing her arms and studying him as if he were her latest science experiment. If said experiment could end up with the pair of them naked, he'd be all for it. But something bigger was at stake. His part in their son's future. For that talk he needed his brain in full working order.

No longer able to bear being the object of her scrutiny, he abruptly started opening and closing cupboards. "You know, the one thing I couldn't find was actual pasta. Where do you keep it hidden in this labyrinth of a kitchen of yours?"

"Ah…" She tapped the side of her nose and lifted a near invisible hatch on to a geriatric dumb waiter. "This is my secret pantry." She swung her hands into a *Ta-da!* pose, then quirked her head to the side. "Oh."

"Secret pantry empty tonight?" Matthew asked drily.

Amanda pushed her lips out into a pouty little moue, then nodded. "It appears so."

"Are there any shops open in this neck of the woods? I can nip out and grab some, if you like."

And ice the urge to rip your clothes off while I'm at it.

Amanda slumped onto a kitchen chair and made a show of slow-motion banging her head on the wooden table. "Why, why, *why* can't one thing go right today?"

Unable to stop himself, he skirted round behind Amanda, pulled her discarded blanket up and round her shoulders. "C'mon. Up you get."

"What? No," she said grumpily into the fold of her arms. "I'm not moving."

"Yes, you are. You're going to sit in this chair, over by the range, and watch the sauce while I nip out and find some pasta."

"I don't want to eat anymore. Not hungry," she pouted, though there was a touch of playfulness about her voice now. And the sound of her tummy audibly disagreeing.

"C'mon, little unicorn. Up you get."

He pulled Amanda's chair away from the table with her still in it, then went round to the front of her and lifted her up to stand, tucking his finger under chin and forcing her to look at him.

"I am not having the mother of my child pass out from hunger. Or get chilblains while she waits for her man to bring back provisions."

Her man?

Where had *that* come from?

Amanda peered up at him, her lower lip protruding like a forlorn child's, before pouting. "If there's garlic bread out there could you get some of that, too?"

If they had been a couple this would have been the moment he would have dropped a delicate kiss on to her lips, followed by another, and another, until his fingers finally took purchase of that zip of hers and he was sliding his hands along her bare—

Amanda's tummy gurgled again. She put up *pretty-please* hands.

He laughed. "I will do my best to hunt and gather some garlic bread."

"Focaccia, if they have it. Not to be fussy or anything." Amanda's lips quirked into a lopsided smile.

Unable to stop himself, he stroked a few errant locks of blond hair back behind her ears, his fingertips grazing the soft down of her cheek as he did.

It would be so easy to fall in love with you.

He cleared his throat and stepped around her. If he wanted to protect and care for her and their so he was going to have to keep his distance. Hopefully the garlic bread would be strong enough to do the trick.

CHAPTER ELEVEN

"YUM." AMANDA PUSHED back her plate and patted her belly with both her hands. "That was delicious. Did your mother teach you to cook like that?"

"No." Matthew screeched his chair back against the tiled floor, swiftly picking up their empty plates and taking them to the sink.

Okaaaay... "Touchy subject?"

"Something like that." Matthew's shoulders tightened as he turned the taps on full and started scrubbing at the dishes.

"Fair enough." She tried to bring back the more relaxed atmosphere the pair of them had enjoyed over supper. Telling work stories mostly.

"My mother is hardly the top of my conversational favorites playlist."

"You have a playlist, do you?"

His shoulders hunched. His actions intensified.

Scrub, scrub, scrub. Stack. Clank. Scrub. Clank. Screech of the tap.

"This water is bloody freezing, Amanda. Is your boiler working?"

A sigh gushed out of Amanda's chest. "It's on the list."

"What list?" Matthew whirled round,

There had been a bit more bite in his voice than she

thought he'd intended. Still more curious than accusatory. But even so… *Pfft*. He didn't look as if he'd leave until he had an answer, so she'd better 'fess up.

"The I'm-always-breaking-so-I-need-to-be-replaced list." She held up a hand and started ticking off on her fingers. "Heating, plumbing, double-glazing. There's more, too. Cooking, shopping…" She threw both of her hands up in despair. "It's never-ending."

The crease between Matthew's eyes deepened. They were glinting a darker blue than she'd ever seen them. A shiver of unease juddered down her spine. He wasn't going to try to sue her for custody, was he? Deem her an unfit mother?

"Is this about money? Is it money you need?"

A baby dragon she hadn't realized had been living in her heart roared to life.

Amanda jumped up from her chair and pointed to the door. "If that's why you think I let you carry my son home you can just take your coat and leave. *Now*."

Matthew tipped his chin to the side, his jaw tightening and his eyes narrowing as he coolly considered her. She watched his Adam's apple as he appeared literally to swallow what she was saying.

"I think," he said, after a taut moment of silence, "you meant *our* son. And I wasn't suggesting you were luring me in here with your feminine wiles to get your hands on my wallet. I was asking if the reason your house hasn't been brought into the twenty-first century is because of a cash flow problem."

Amanda felt her indignation deflate like a popped balloon. "Oh. Right. Um…" She scrunched her mouth into a wince. "Sorry."

"Well?" Matthew persisted. "Is it?"

"Is it what? About money? Yes. It's about money. But not yours. I work hard for everything I have, and I learned long ago that other people's money comes with conditions. And, no. Before you say it, I can't ask my parents. I can see it in your eyes. Why isn't Daddy helping? I'm afraid it's a big, fat boo-hoo for the poor little rich girl. Daddy found out she wasn't the pure, innocent little thing he wanted her to be so he yanked her trust fund away. Rightfully so, in case you're wondering. And, yes—it was a *long* time ago. Well before I met you."

"But I thought—"

"What? That because we were all at that benefit together we were a happy little family?"

Matthew nodded.

"Wrong again. That was for show. They were putting me through my paces—seeing if I could be crammed back into one of their precious little society roles. A trial run for the chastened daughter, I suppose. And guess what?" She rounded her hands in front of her belly as if she were pregnant again. "I failed."

"You had Tristan to make your parents angry?" Matthew looked genuinely confused.

Feeling more of an idiot than a triumphant speech-giver, Amanda gave an exasperated toss of her hair and "deflated" her stomach. Frankly, she was a bit shocked at herself. Stunned, really. What was she doing, telling Matthew so much? Then it hit her. She *wanted* to tell him.

She'd been carrying around the weight of wondering whether or not to tell Matthew about his son for nearly three years and finally—explosively—she had a chance to unload it. *All* of it. She'd braced herself all this time for stormy rage and rejection, but…astonishingly…he was just standing there listening, nodding, taking what she said on board. Digesting.

He wasn't looking thrilled, exactly, but... In for a penny, in for a pound. He wanted to know who the mother of his child was? He was going to hear the whole blinking story in all its gory details.

"C'mon." She pulled the blanket from the back of the chair and headed toward the central corridor. "Let's go into the sitting room. You'll need to get comfortable for this."

She walked into the high-ceilinged room and pulled the heavy drapes tight—then abruptly changed her mind when she saw how beautiful the falling snow was and pushed them open again.

"Shall I build a fire?" Matthew asked from the doorway.

"I should've bought a Christmas tree."

Amanda sighed as she turned around and saw the room for what it was. A sitting room yet to acknowledge the holidays.

"Fire?" Matthew asked again, pointedly ignoring her Christmas tree comment.

What *was* it with him and Christmas anyway? She *loved* it. Just hadn't gotten round to decorating. Or gift shopping.

"Amanda? Fire?"

"Yes, please." She pointed to the wood stove her aunt had installed when she'd moved in over thirty years earlier. It still chugged along like a steam engine, but was no match for modern-day heating.

"Matches?"

"On the shelf there—with the photos on it."

Matthew scanned the shelf and instead of picking up the matches picked up the photo in a small silver frame her aunt had insisted upon putting in the sitting room. Protesting, as she'd learned shortly after moving in, was pointless.

"Is this you with…?"

"Yup." She nodded, a flush of heat pinking up her cheeks. "That's me at… I think I was eight months pregnant."

She didn't know why she'd pretended to sound unsure. She knew exactly when it was. The day she'd moved in with her aunt after the head of the A&E department she'd been running had insisted she start taking her maternity leave straight away. In the highly strung state she'd been in she'd told them to take their job and stuff it. And they had.

More fodder for her belief that the whole world was out to prove she wasn't mature enough to handle responsibility. Now she had a bit more perspective. She saw that they'd been looking after her interests as much as their own. But that didn't mean the wound still didn't have a bit of sting left in it.

"You look beautiful," Matthew whispered, then met her gaze with a soft smile. "I wish I'd…"

He let the sentence trail off and pressed his lips into a tight line. They were both old enough to know that wishing didn't make dreams come true.

"I'm sorry I didn't tell you," she blurted.

"Why didn't you? Really."

He sat down on the far end of the sofa, one leg bent and the other hooked over it, a scarlet throw pillow peeking out from behind his back. Funny how at home he seemed in this old house. Some people didn't quite know how to behave in it, with its eclectic collection of antiques and plain old well-loved furniture.

Museum or madhouse? A bit of both, really, if you included Florence and herself. Tristan was the only sane member of the family.

Tristan. The entire reason the two of them were here tonight.

She forced herself to meet Matthew's blue-eyed gaze.

"I suppose…" She knew she owed Matthew the truth. "I suppose I wanted something all of my own. Someone I could love without conditions. Someone I could show on a daily basis that I was worth loving, too."

She could have gone on, but the build-up of admitting even that much made her want to pull the blanket over her head and run upstairs to her room. But she had to do this. For Tristan. If his father wanted to be in his life, to show him the love he deserved, she needed to find a way to let Matthew in.

"What happened with your parents?" he asked. "It was them, wasn't it? Who made you feel you weren't worthy of love?"

"Sort of. Mostly. Or maybe it was me. But if you want me to pick one single incident when my parents made it clear I wasn't up to snuff for being a 'proper Wakehurst' I don't think I could."

It was impossible to keep the strain of bitterness from her laugh, but just as quickly it slipped away. Holding on to that level of anger wasn't going to help anyone— least of all her son, whom she hoped would get to meet his grandparents one day. How would they be able to resist those chubby little cheeks of his and those bright baby blues?

Perhaps it was time to turn the anger to sadness and then, if she could, let the sadness heal. Put out an olive branch. Swallow her pride and try again. At the end of the day she would never be at peace if she didn't put things right with her mother and father.

"Sometimes I think that no matter *who* a person is all their issues always boil down to dear ol' Mum and Dad, don't they?"

She'd said it more as a filler, but Matthew's response—a slow, weighted nod—showed just how true it was.

"Okay." She huffed out a sigh, then warned him, "The whole story might take a while."

Matthew opened his palms toward her in an I've-got-all-the-time-in-the-world gesture.

"Right." She put up her index finger. "Let me just say, right off the bat, that I know mine is hardly a tragic tale, but it does explain how Lady Amanda the trust fund princess became a doctor, then a single mum and has been trying to get her act together ever since."

"I don't see you like that."

A soft warmth fluttered in her heart as Matthew's confused expression turned almost defensive. As if he were protecting her from the pain her memories caused.

Swoon!

Regroup.

He's not tilting his lance for you.

Yet.

Big breath in. "So...my childhood was your typical rich kid's."

"I didn't have one of those. I'm afraid you're going to have to spell it out for me."

She widened her eyes in surprise. He seemed so at ease with his wealth. The charitable giving... His offers to help her with the wretched heating in this old house...

"But your father's company—"

"Became successful after..." Matthew paused, his eyes growing as dark as a fathomless sea. "His company took off once I'd left home."

Amanda was tempted to urge Matthew to tell *his* story,

but his demeanor had shifted from I've-Got-All-Night to Just-Get-On-With-It.

"In my case it involved lots of nannies. They were always quitting, claiming I was a bit of a handful. And I guess I was." She laughed thinking of the time she copied one of the tricks out of *The Parent Trap* involving honey and lots of string. It had seemed funny at the time.

"Usual naughty pranks?"

"Got it in one." Amanda gave him a thumbs-up. "If I were a psychiatrist I would probably chalk it up to attention-seeking. My parents were always away at parties, or hiding me away from their guests when they entertained at home. Then there was boarding school, when they grew tired of holding interviews for new nannies. During the holidays I was trotted out and expected to…" She looked up to the ceiling, searching for the perfect word. "*Perform*, I guess."

"What? Like a circus animal? 'Show us your tricks, you clever girl?'"

Matthew's eyes had widened in disbelief. It looked as if *his* parents hadn't gone down that route.

"Pretty much," Amanda answered, suddenly remembering the conversations she'd been forced to have in French, and later Italian, with visiting guests from the continent. "I guess all that performing on demand stuff brought out the rebel in me. That and my parents were never home long enough to take a blind bit of notice of the fact that their daughter was turning into a hellion."

Matthew smiled. "I would've enjoyed seeing Amanda the hellion."

The light drained from her heart at all the bad memories.

"No. You wouldn't have." She folded her hands together and stared at them as she continued. "I partied a lot. Too much. I was studying pre-med, but I found things easy enough that running away at weekends to drown myself in Cosmos or G&Ts or whatever the drink of the moment was seemed like a good thing. A fun thing…"

"Until…?"

She looked up and met his inquisitive gaze.

My God, he has beautiful eyes. And when he learns this about me they'll be filled with scorn and he will leave me too.

Her heart cinched tight. Not telling him would have the same effect. And she needed to give Tristan the chance to have a father. If being a father was what Matthew wanted.

"One weekend things went well beyond crazy. I had a trust fund. A big one. My friends had much the same and we—we jumped on a plane and went to Las Vegas."

"Sounds expensive, but it doesn't sound like the worst thing in the world." Matthew leaned forward and put a hand on her knee. "Why are you still beating yourself up about it?"

She looked at his hand, doing her best to ignore the warmth shifting from his body to hers. As she spoke she watched his fingers, waiting for their response to what she said next.

"I got married."

And there goes the comforting hand.

Matthew sat back on the sofa as he took in the news, but to his credit he didn't look judgmental. Just curious.

"And your husband…?"

"He was a nice enough guy. Older than me by a few years. In the British army."

She only just stopped herself from giving him a wink and saying that therefore Matthew was obviously her type. But John and Matthew were worlds apart.

"He was on leave and undecided about whether or not to sign up for another tour or retire and start the specialty car repair garage he'd always talked about with a couple of his mates."

Darkness began to shadow her heart. He hadn't been that bad. And he'd only slapped her just the once. But once had been enough for her to say what she really thought of him once her rose-colored glasses had shattered.

She swallowed and forced herself to continue, barely recognizing her own voice as she explained, "He knew I was a trust fund kid and—unbeknownst to me at the time—he saw me as a way to not have to work for a living. Just…party. Fund his garage. Buy a cool car. But when we got back my father went ballistic. He put a stop on my accounts. Took all my credit cards. Said if I was old enough to get married I was old enough to look after myself. My mother was… She looked absolutely disgusted when I told her what I'd done."

"Tough love?" Matthew said, as the silence in the room demanded filling.

"Something like that." She kept on talking, because she only wanted to tell this story once. "Once John found out I was no longer rolling in it a whole different side to him came out. A mean one. He drank—but not for fun."

"Why did he drink?"

Matthew's jaw tightened, and again she saw his hackles rise on her behalf. The empathy that shone from his eyes gave her the courage to tell him the horrible things she would have willingly had erased from her mind if she'd been able to.

"The truth?"

Matthew nodded. That was what they were here for.

"He wanted to drown out the fact that he'd married a

university student who still had five more years of medical school to attend before she earned so much as a penny. I was still young enough—arrogant enough—to believe I had been put on this earth to be a doctor and I wasn't going to settle for anything less. I told him if he wanted to live off me once I was working he'd have to put some graft in too. Sign up for another tour in the army while I carried on at med school. He resisted. I became more insistent. The fights grew meaner. Angrier. He told me the only reason I was in med school at all was because my parents had given millions to the university. That the uni had *had* to take me so they could flaunt the Wakehurst name."

Her shoulders slumped at the memory. She'd worked so hard to get in. And even harder to get out. To prove she was as valid a candidate as anyone else.

"And then one day we fought so bitterly he hit me."

Her hand flew to her cheek, as if reliving the moment. It hadn't been the pain so much as the shock. Outside of her parents, no one had ever treated her as if she were so insignificant…worthless. Unfit to be loved. And John had repeated each and every one of those things until he'd all but ground them into her very cell structure.

When Matthew finally spoke his voice came out as a growl. "Where is he now?"

Amanda looked up at him, tears falling freely from her eyes, and said the only thing she could. "Dead."

His expression remained unchanged. "How?"

"I'd told him he was useless. That a real man would go out and work instead of getting drunk and hitting his wife, and the next morning he was gone. He signed up for another tour and a few weeks later…" A sob escaped her throat but she forced herself to finish. "There was a knock at the door."

"Killed in action?"

She nodded, too tired to spell it out. Matthew was smart, and he had been in war zones himself. He knew how these things went.

"My parents were still refusing to see me, so I threw myself into med school. I couldn't get enough of it. Treating patients was a way of dealing with my own grief."

"Did you love him?" Matthew asked softly.

Amanda shook her head. "Of course I thought I did at first, but once the cocktails wore off and the money dried up reality hit like a two-ton lorry. It was obvious to just about everyone—including me—that we'd made a massive mistake. If things hadn't ended the way they did I have no doubt I'd be a divorcee instead of a widow."

She could have dealt with that. But carrying the guilt that her words had sent John to a war he'd never returned from... She'd barely been able to look his parents in the eye at the funeral. And they'd made it more than clear that she wasn't welcome at the wake.

Throwing her energies into work, doing her best to help people at their weakest, most frightened moments, seemed the only way to try and make amends.

"How did you and your parents come to mend fences for the SoS ball?"

"Ha!" Amanda surprised herself by cackling—a counterbalance to the raw, searing pain of admitting how her reckless behavior had led to such a horrible turn of events. "When I got a job running an A&E in Chelsea they thought it was okay to trot me out amongst their crowd again. And by then I didn't really care. I was... I was completely numb until—"

"Until?" Matthew leant forward again.

Amanda's breath caught in her throat when she looked up, and her gaze meshed with Matthew's so perfectly she wondered how fate could have been so generous as to have put Matthew in her life. Given her her precious son.

"Until I met you."

CHAPTER TWELVE

MATTHEW'S HEART EXPLODED in his chest.

Hope clashed with fear as his brain caught up with the rapid flow of events to remind himself he wasn't a safe bet. He didn't do commitment. But when Amanda had told him her husband had hit her... He'd known damn straight that he'd go to bat for her any day of the week. Even if meant risking his heart.

Was that what this was? The heart pounding in his chest? The blood pumping through his veins with a vigor—a lightness—he hadn't felt before? Was he actually letting himself fall in love?

"The charity ball was a...a very nice night." He eventually allowed.

"That's putting it mildly." Amanda stretched her leg out and gave him a playful shove on the knee, but not two seconds later the light left her eyes. "When I saw you it was like coming out of a coma."

"With you looking so miserable, I don't know if it that's a good thing or a bad thing," Matthew joked, only to receive another play-kick.

"It was very good thing...even if it *did* cost me."

"Cost you how?"

"Oh...my parents didn't like my decision. They thought my keeping Tristan was like wearing a scarlet A—proof I

had never really grown out of my wild-child phase and…"
She looked up at him, an unexpected hint of naughtiness
sparkling in her eyes. "I suppose with the right man rip-
ping my dress off there *is* a side of me I can't control.
Not that there have been heaps of them. Men, I mean,"
she quickly qualified. "You were kind of a… You were
a One Night Only special."

Matthew tried to contain the swell of pride he felt
as Amanda made it clear he had as strong an effect on
her as she did on him. Tonight wasn't about bolstering
his ego. It was about Amanda. And their son. She was
trusting him with her darkest memories, and instead of
running for the hills he knew in his heart he wanted to
honor them. Honor *her*.

She worked hard. Had obviously turned her life around
on her own. Yes, she had her aunt, but she hadn't come
to him begging for hand-outs— *Ah. That was why she
hadn't told him.* She'd wanted to prove to herself she
could do it on her own because her parents and her husband had made her believe she was worthless. Capable
of nothing.

"And calling me to tell me you were pregnant would
have meant risking another rejection?"

Amanda smiled shyly. "You should've been a shrink,
Dr. Chase. Or a mind reader."

"Let's just say I have a rough idea where you're coming from."

She raised her eyebrows, her curiosity clearly piqued.
But she didn't press. And he was grateful to her for that.
On top of the whole discovering he had a son thing he
was just about covered on the "things to mull over" front
for the foreseeable future. No doubt about it.

But his heart was going against the tide, insisting he

already knew what to do. Get to know this woman. Cherish her. Love her. Protect her. And Tristan, too.

But he was built of history, and history dictated that he wasn't the man for the job. Giving Amanda what was best might not be the fairy tale ending she was hoping for—but he'd find a way to help.

He watched as Amanda's body became consumed by a yawn—one of those head-to-toe numbers that only came from emotional exhaustion.

"Looks like someone needs their bed." He stood up and offered her his hand.

She took it and rose, looked him squarely in the eye and shook her head. "Can't. I've got to let Auntie Florence get some sleep. Concussion Watch continues."

"Let me do it."

Amanda looked as shocked as he felt by the offer. And then another full-body yawn rippled through her.

"Go on." He turned her around and gave her a gentle nudge toward the door, only just resisting giving her pert derriere a short caress as she took a step on to the stairs. "Show me the way and I'll stay with Tristan."

The name felt unfamiliar, but sweet on his tongue. *Tristan*. His little knight.

Amanda shot him a dubious look, but after a quick eye-scrunch eventually shrugged, as if to say, *Okay, whatever you want*, and started shuffling up the stairs in her big fluffy slippers.

He stood out in the corridor while he heard her murmuring an explanation to her aunt. When Florence came out of the room she didn't say anything, but pressed her hand to his forearm, gave it a squeeze and gave him a nod, as if a future between him and Amanda was a done deal.

As Florence walked up another swirl of stairs to her

room he was struck by how—in just those few tiny moments—he'd felt more a part of a family than he had since
his brother had died.

"Right. You ready?" Amanda poked her head out of
the dark bedroom and waved him in, keeping her voice
low. "He's still sleeping, but his vitals are all checking
out well. No signs of anything other than a tired little boy
with a bit of a gash on his head."

Matthew stood by Amanda, looking down at the
small figure tucked into a low trundle bed beneath a
navy duvet, surrounded by soft toys and books. Curly
hair had gone haywire on the pillow. Small hands were
clutching a well-loved rabbit.

His son.

The swell of emotion in his chest grew so tight it was
almost painful. Was *this* what love at first sight truly
was? A parent's love for their child?

He wondered how his own parents had found it so easy
to forget that *he'd* still needed love after Charlie died.
Not seeing how their silent looks and cold words had all
but killed his own will to live. Looking at his own son
now, he was grateful he had turned the cold, isolated
pain and guilt of his childhood into a burning desire to
do one good thing.

Tristan—he knew it in the very center of his soul—
was his one good thing.

"C'mere." He sat down on the chaise longue, leaving one leg on the floor. "Use me as your pillow. Watch
your son for a bit."

Amanda gave him a well-deserved wary look. Com-
ponents of his personality he'd never known existed kept
leaping to the fore. The gallant gent. The astonished father. The caring husb— *No.* They weren't anywhere close
to that yet, but…

He gave her arm a reassuring rub. "I won't bite. And you deserve a rest."

Still giving him a wary sidelong glance, she lowered herself to the upholstered base, throwing him a hesitant look over her shoulder. "This is a bit weird."

He nodded. "I know. For tonight, shall we just pretend it's normal?"

Again the dubious look. "We don't *have* a 'normal.'"

"True." He beckoned with his hands for her to join him. "Doesn't mean we can't start making one."

"Yeah, right." She sniggered. "You and me? Normal?"

"Stranger things have happened."

Like him being possessed by The Guy Who Wants to Stick Around, for starters.

Amanda suppressed another yawn.

"Okay, sleepy bear." He scooched further back on the chaise to make more room. "Don't fight nature. Lean back and watch your son."

Amanda began to, and then abruptly whirled around, pointing an accusatory finger. "No hanky-panky."

He laughed. "What we got up to was *not* hanky-panky."

The air instantly thickened between them.

Amanda's eyelids cloaked her hazel irises for a moment, before opening to show him he hadn't been the only one reliving that night.

"No hanky-panky," she whispered.

He crossed his heart. "I'm not saying the thought hasn't crossed my mind, but tonight I vow not to ravage every delicious curve of your body."

"Delicious?" She quirked an eyebrow, as if it was a complete revelation that he had something nice to say about her sensuality.

Off the charts wasn't even close to describing how he thought of her.

"Michelin-starred delicious," he confirmed soberly. "Never had better."

"Oh. Well…" She rearranged her surprise into a playful of-course-I-was face and finally leaned back against him, as if the topic were now a signed and sealed deal. No hanky-panky for tonight… But in the future? *To be determined.*

He smiled as she settled back, remarkably pleased that they were adding yet another layer to their relationship. Was this what being content…*happy*…was all about?

Amanda held herself rigidly at first, and then, as their breathing began to match each other's, his fingers weaving between hers and twisting into a folding of arms and hands across her belly, Matthew felt her begin to genuinely relax against him, ultimately letting her full weight rest against his chest until eventually, to the steady beat of his heart, she fell asleep.

At that moment Matthew knew there was *another* good thing he could do, and he prayed with all his might that he'd have the courage to do the second.

Amanda stretched and yawned like a well-rested cat, hardly able to remember when she'd slept so well. She rolled to her side, delighted to see the tree branches outside her window were hidden beneath a thick layer of snow. She fell back onto her pile of pillows and grinned.

And then her mind caught up with the unfamiliar sensations of feeling protected and cared for. And in her bed. Hadn't she fallen asleep on the chaise longue? With Matthew?

Her eyes popped open.

Matthew was downstairs with her son.

She pulled a dressing gown over her onesie, rammed her feet into her unicorn slippers and virtually skied down the stairwell, first to Tristan's room—which was empty—and then to the kitchen, where she heard the low rumble of Matthew's voice and also...

She screeched to a halt and forced herself to listen outside the kitchen door.

Tristan's laughter.

She pressed her ear to the swing door, doing her best not to set it swinging.

"And in that hospital he had a...stethoscope...e-i-e-i-o."

Was Matthew singing a medical version of "Old Mac-Donald"? She pressed her fingers to her lips to stop herself from giggling. Tristan, from the sounds of things, found his version of the age-old song as hilarious as she did.

"With a tachycardia here and a pulmonary there...here a beat...there a beat...everywhere a beat-beat."

When she heard her son's peal of laughter chased up by, "More!" she could no longer resist having a peek.

She gently pressed the door open to see Tristan sitting in a chair opposite Matthew, who was standing up and beginning a rendition of "Head, Shoulders, Knees and Toes" and getting Tristan to mimic him as he pointed out the body areas.

"Mummy!" Tristan virtually leapt off his chair and raced to her, putting his arms snugly and securely around her legs.

Amanda eased herself down into a squat and pulled him into her arms, eventually falling back onto the kitchen floor in a full-on cuddle session.

She looked up to see Matthew silently but warmly taking in the scene. It felt strange to have him watching something so...not intimate, exactly, but... Yes. It was intimate. Tristan had been hers and hers alone to protect, and yet after pouring her heart out to Matthew last night, and not feeling a moment's judgment from him, this felt...*natural*. And still a little bit weird.

She tightened her hold around Tristan and sat up, holding him back from her so she could look at his cut. "You've put on a fresh dressing."

Matthew turned toward the range. "I thought you wouldn't mind. He woke up early and I wanted to have a look. Run some tests."

"Tests?"

"Nothing serious, Mum," he said gently, slipping his hands into her aunt's floral oven gloves. He turned them into puppets when he noticed Tristan watching. "Just wanted to check everything was all right with Tristan."

Amanda glanced at Tristan, who seemed enthralled by Matthew's puppet hands. She traced her thumb along the edges of her toddler's face. "Looks like he's going to have a nice set of black eyes."

"Yes," Matthew said in a goofy voice, still using the oven glove hand puppets, "but nothing else to worry about except a bit of itching when that cut begins to heal."

Tristan put his hands on his head, the same as Matthew. An entirely new swirl of emotions swept through Amanda. This was all well and good—the happy families thing—but if Matthew wasn't going to stick around was it worth encouraging?

She picked up Tristan with a small groan. "Oof! You're getting heavy, little one."

"He's a good-looking boy." Matthew said, his attention on pulling open one of the range's doors.

Amanda looked at Matthew's backside and thought she'd be giving it a swat if she were close enough. Of *course* he was a good-looking boy. Matthew was absolutely gorgeous. Anything that sprang from his gene pool would be…

Screech!

Stop thinking like that. You will not be having more babies with Matthew Chase. Or anyone.

"*Croissant, mademoiselle?*"

Her eyes widened as Matthew revealed a tray of steaming hot croissants and slid them onto the counter alongside a pot of strawberry preserve she hadn't remembered buying. "Where did you—?"

"Tristan and I went for a little shop after we popped into the hospital, didn't we?"

Her son nodded obligingly, then reached toward the croissants.

"They're hot, darling," Amanda trapped his little hand in her own and popped a kiss on his knuckles, fighting the urge to tell Matthew off for kidnapping. "Why don't you go climb onto your chair and Mummy will get you some milk while they cool down?"

She walked round the counter, mouthing *Hospital?* to Matthew, who shrugged.

"I just wanted to make sure."

"Sure of what?" Amanda hissed, anxiety rising up her throat like a temperature gauge in a pot of boiling sugar. Tristan was *her* son. She'd looked after him for the past—

Calm, calm, calm. The man was a doctor after all.

"Tristan! Croissant!" her son called out, in a noisy campaign to get his groping hands on one of the warm pastries as soon as possible.

"Yes, darling, your fa—" She stopped again and looked at Matthew. "I don't know what to call you."

A flash of something she couldn't put her finger on shadowed Matthew's blue eyes. Pain. Regret?

Okay. Baby steps. This is all new to him.

"What have you had him call you this morning?" she asked.

Matthew shook his head. "Nothing, really. We've just been working on buying croissants and learning anatomy."

"Matthew." She threw him a disbelieving look. "He's two."

"I'm well aware of how old he is." Matthew gave her a wicked smile. "Believe it or not, I remember the night he was conceived as vividly as you do. And, unlike Tristan, I can count."

Amanda's hackles flew up. "*He* can count!"

"Amanda, I am teasing. I know where a two-year-old should be on the developmental scale as well as you do. I went to med school. Remember?"

"You certainly don't sound like you're teasing." Her hands flew to her hips and then she felt ridiculous, so she crossed them over her chest as if it would stop her heart pounding so hard.

He's just trying to do his best. And he made it possible for you to have the best sleep you've had in years. In his arms.

Amanda's stomach tightened against the complex emotions set loose in her mind. A whirling tornado of hopes and fears culminated in one question on a loop: How can I tell him I want him to stay? That I want Tristan to call him Daddy?

Matthew busied himself wiping up invisible crumbs, offering himself grim congratulations for not suggesting their son call him Uncle Matthew. It was the first thing that had popped into his mind, but he knew it wasn't right. Amanda would see the moniker for what it was. A cop-out. A way to keep his distance. A means of walking away.

"Would you be all right with 'esteemed paternal figure'?" he asked, only to receive a gale force glare. "Daddy?" That was even worse.

Tristan hadn't heard as he had taken up singing the "Head, Shoulders" song again. Thank heavens. And a good sign he hadn't received any additional injuries beyond the superficial.

Of course it had been excessive to sneak him into the hospital for another round of scans. He'd made sure the hospital charged him for the tests, but even so...was he already a helicopter father? Unable to follow his own medical advice? *Wait and see. Watch and listen.* Or was he a dedicated singleton who'd just found out he had a son and was climbing the steepest learning curve a man could climb?

Amanda was fishing enough for him to tell she was as confused as he was.

"Why don't we go with 'Matthew' for the next few days?" he tried, ducking his head to try and see if he could get her to look him in the eye. "To make things easier."

"How early did you go to the hospital, anyhow?" Amanda answered his question with another.

He felt a strange hit of relief that she was as discombobulated as he was. As if they'd both been hit by a tidal wave of information and were only just beginning to sort through the pieces, bit by bit, problem by problem.

"It's ten o'clock. We've been up for hours."

"Ten!" Amanda screeched, eyes widening, hands scrubbing through her hair. "We were meant to be at the hospital at seven. Why didn't you wake me?"

Matthew laughed softly, reaching out a hand to rub her shoulder.

She shook him off with an angry shake of her head. "We're meant to be at work."

"It's Saturday, love. We're not rostered on."

Amanda stopped, her expression frozen in place as her mind whirled and then rapidly put the pieces together.

Matthew was becoming more familiar with her little quirks now. Racing to conclusions. Stopping when she discovered things weren't as she'd thought. Processing. Forming a tactical response. It was cute. *She* was cute. Hell. Who was he kidding? She was gorgeous and a brainbox to boot. It had taken his deepest reserves of willpower not to slip into bed with her when he'd carried her to her room.

"You just called me 'love'," Amanda snapped.

Okay. Not quite the response he was expecting.

"I call a lot of people 'love.'"

"Well, then," Amanda sniffed, giving him a little up-down *wrong answer* scan. "I think we'd better stick to 'Matthew' until we figure out how we're going to work things out."

"Tristan *hungry*!"

"Of course, love."

Matthew smiled as Amanda flinched at her own use of the word and flew into action. Strangely, the moment confirmed that he was right to be here, right to try and work out how they would tackle things. Mistakes and all. Together.

As Amanda fussed about, getting a plate and a butter knife, he crossed his arms over his chest and leaned against the warm range as she briskly picked up one of the croissants and brought the strawberry preserve over to Tristan.

"I've got an idea," he said, once she'd set up his breakfast and a wobbly bottomed beaker of milk with a sippy top.

"You seem to be full of them this morning."

"Hey, now…"

Even though Amanda tensed as he pulled her into his arms he continued to hold her, running his fingers through her hair, rubbing a hand along her back, until eventually she melted into him…a little bit.

"I know I'm the odd man out here, but we've got to sort out how we want to do things one day. Why not start with this weekend?"

She looked up at him, hair all tousled from sleep, eyes wide with equal washes of hope and disbelief.

"What do you say I go home and grab a few things and then, only if you're happy with it, I stay here—or in one of the doctors' rooms at the hospital—and we spend time together…as a family?"

Amanda bristled, wriggling out of his embrace. "I don't think we can just leap into double-barreling our names, Matthew."

"I am well aware of that. But I'm also aware that if you don't spend time with family it's easy enough to behave as if you don't have one."

"What exactly are you saying?" She glanced across at Tristan, then lowered her voice to a whisper. "My parents *chose* not to be part of our lives. I don't think it's fair to judge me for their decision."

"I'm not talking about your family, Amanda. I'm talking about mine."

If his childhood had taught him anything, it was that being part of a family, even with its intense, often painful emotional peaks and troughs, took work and stamina and bottomless wells of effort. And, while Amanda might not want him in their day-to-day lives, he was never going to let Tristan feel as alone as he had.

"Oh, well…" Amanda pulled back another step and began tracing figure eights on the marble counter-top. "Is this the part where I need to ask you about your past so we're on even territory?" She tilted her head to the side and made a goofy face. "Should we have a Who's Got the Nuttiest Family contest?"

"No." Matthew bit off the word and turned away from Amanda's shocked expression at his terse response. "Where do you keep your coffee? Or are you more of a tea girl?"

"Tea," she answered cautiously.

After a moment he felt her touch her fingers to his arm.

"Matthew, do you want to speak about your parents? Not now," she added quickly. "But it kind of sounds like you've got some cupboards that need airing."

"No more than the next guy," he responded, with a practiced cover-up-the-darkness smile. "Look. I obviously jumped the gun on the whole spending the weekend together thing. What do you say we spend the day together instead? Build up to a weekend. Maybe…"

He racked his brain for something a family with a toddler did.

"How would you feel about going to Hyde Park?" Amanda asked.

"The park? Sure. Sounds great. We can see the mounted brigade ride their horses. Tristan would love that—wouldn't you, mate?"

Amanda shot him a sideways look, her teeth capturing her bottom lip as if she were trying to stop herself from commenting.

Mate? Had he just called his son *mate?* What kind of an idiot did that? A father? Luckily Tristan was too engrossed in a picture book with a clown nose he could honk on each page to notice.

"I was thinking something more along the lines of the Christmas village. There are all sorts of rides and ice sculptures."

Amanda could obviously see the doubt in his eyes, because she'd put on her best sell-it-big voice.

"They have ice skating and mulled wine—"

"Oh, are you taking Tristan to see Santa?"

Florence appeared at the kitchen doorway, tugging the belt of her floral dressing gown tight and not looking the least bit surprised to find Matthew there in yesterday's clothes.

"Does this mean our toddling hero, here, is all right?"

Grateful for Florence's appearance, Amanda diverted her attention to her son and her aunt.

Matthew made cups of tea and wondered how on earth he'd gone from being a tried and true bachelor to almost baring his soul to the one woman in the world who had come closest to wrenching open the door to what remained of his tattered heart.

There was a part of him that hoped she would stick her foot in that door, demand he open it. Be as brave and honest as she had been last night. But there was another, more powerful part that knew when she looked in and saw all the pieces of history that made him whole she'd turn and walk away.

He would. But for this weekend he would suck it up. Put aside his hatred of Christmas and tinsel and twinkly lights. He was going to have *fun*. Even if it ate him alive inside while he was doing it.

"While we're at it…" he handed a cup of tea to Florence, then met Amanda's inquisitive gaze "…why don't we get this house a Christmas tree?"

CHAPTER THIRTEEN

"WAIT. HANG ON a minute."

Amanda stopped and turned to Matthew, just about ready to step onto the ice rink with Tristan and his ride-on reindeer. She squeezed his little hand in hers as her she met Matthew's gaze, her ankles wobbling just the tiniest bit in her ice skates. There was a softness in Matthew's expression she wouldn't have expected to see after a full day with a toddler. Particularly one who was refusing to take a nap.

"Mummy! Reindeer!"

Amanda heard her son. Felt the tug on her hand. But she stood completely bewitched by the beautiful blue of Matthew's eyes. He was looking at her so *intently*.

"Just a minute, love."

The blood rushing round her head was drowning out her own voice, and she barely knew if she was speaking to Tristan or Matthew. Their day of carrousel rides, gingerbread men, ice sculptures and even glimpses of the mounted cavalry in Hyde Park had passed in a whirl of adrenaline and laughter.

"Don't move." Matthew's voice was low, reserved for the little bubble of perfection that was forming round them.

As if she could! She even had to reach out to the side

of the rink and hold on to give her knees some extra support. Was he going to kiss her? In front of Tristan? The whole of London?

Her heart began thumping. No doubt her pupils were dilating. She felt giddier than she ever had. Like an innocent teenage girl about to receive her first kiss. Matthew's eyes slipped from hers as the tip of her tongue swept the length of her lower lip.

Cringe! Now he knew she wanted it. Wanted *him*. *Think*.

Matthew reached out a hand toward her. Was he going to stroke the back of his hand along her cheek? Cup her face in his hands as he pulled her closer toward him?

Think faster!

How far could she let this whirlwind fairy tale day go? Far enough to let herself believe that in less than twenty-four hours she was tumbling head over heels in love with the father of her child? That the desire she'd felt for him all those years ago was burning more strongly than before?

"There," Matthew said at last, swiping the tip of his index finger just below her eye, then pressing his thumb against it. "Eyelash," he said. "Make a wish."

Astonished to feel her heart plummeting from her throat to her toes at the absence of a Winter Wonderland kiss, Amanda gave herself a sharp telling-off and forced a smile and a laugh.

"Go on," Matthew urged. "What would you most like for Christmas?"

You.

Amanda closed her eyes against the dream, sucked in a deep breath and did the only thing she could…wished for a Christmas miracle.

* * *

Matthew hardly recognized himself. He of Great Grinch status was merrily shouldering a seven-foot Christmas tree across a Bedford Square with a beautiful woman by his side and his son—his *son*—half asleep on her shoulder.

He'd noticed how quiet Amanda had become after the eyelash incident and wondered if she was beginning to have second thoughts about this whole "happy families" charade they'd been playing out all day.

The thought shifted and scraped against his conscience.

That wasn't fair and it wasn't accurate. They had been happy—had genuinely enjoyed themselves. They just weren't a family. Not yet anyway.

He glanced over at Amanda, who was digging into her pocket for her keys.

"All right?"

"Yes," she whispered, "Just trying to get the keys without disturbing Tris."

"Here." Matthew leant the tree against the side of the house, surprised to notice it was already gathering its own layer of snowflakes. "I'll take him."

"Are you sure?" Amanda's brow crinkled slightly and her arm tightened ever so slightly against Tristan's back.

"Only if you're happy for me to hold him."

"Of course." She shook her head, as if trying to shake away any concerns she might have. "I'm just so used to doing everything on my own, I—"

A deep ache took hold of Matthew's heart. Amanda worked so hard and gave so much…it was unfair that she had shouldered so much responsibility on her own. Instead of anger that she hadn't told him earlier he felt

shame. Sorrow, even, that he had come across as someone who wouldn't care. Who wouldn't be there.

And that, he thought grimly as he held out his hands
to accept the weight of their son, was the crux of the matter. He was going to have to step up. Make himself into
someone who could be relied on.

"What about the tree?" Amanda moved to the side as
Matthew stepped in, gently wiping the snowflakes from
Tristan's loose curls.

"I'll get it after I put Tristan down."

"I'm not even sure where the decorations are…"
Amanda's top teeth took hold of her bottom lip as she
shot him an apprehensive look.

He could see she still wasn't sure about him. How
much to let him into their lives—if at all. And the ache
of that uncertainty formed into a resolve to do everything he could to be part of their lives—even if he had to
do it from the sidelines. He wanted to be there. Be *here*.

He managed to tug his lips into a smile and nodded
toward the kitchen.

"Why don't you put the kettle on? Get yourself warmed
up? I'll bring the tree inside. It'll need to dry out a bit before being decorated anyway. Perhaps we could meet up
for a hot chocolate and a bit of decorating tomorrow?"

Amanda's shoulders dropped—an instant sign that
he'd made the right call. To back off.

"Amanda darling, is that you?"

They both turned toward the staircase, then threw
anxious looks at Tristan. They needn't have been worried. He was fast asleep, fingers tightly clutching the re-
maining half of the gingerbread heart he'd chosen over
all the Santas and snowmen on offer.

"Here." Matthew handed over his son, vividly aware
that he knew where the other half of that heart was. Not

inside Tristan's little belly, but thumping loudly inside his chest, banging against his ribcage so hard he almost had to catch his breath. "I'll let you two settle him in. Relax for the night."

He hesitated a moment, then went with his gut and dropped a soft kiss on Amanda's forehead. When he pulled back he stroked his hand along Tristan's soft curls and met Amanda's gaze, unsurprised to find her expression completely indecipherable.

"Night, then. I'll give you a ring tomorrow."

She nodded, her eyes watching him as he walked back to the door, opened it up to the magical wintry scene beyond and then pulled it shut behind him.

A sensation of complete emptiness filled him as the door's weighted click sounded against the muted noises of the city. And for the first time in his life Matthew's feet felt leaden, unwilling to take first one step then another toward the solitary, scarcely furnished flat he had once seen as his sanctuary.

He should be in there. Helping out. Tucking his boy in. Helping with supper. Carrying Amanda up to her room and making love to her. And then again for good measure.

But that click of the door had said its piece. He wasn't one of them.

Refusing to let himself turn back on the off chance there would be a final glimpse of Amanda and Tristan in the window, he hunched his shoulders against the cold and headed for the only other place he knew that would provide some form of comfort. The hospital. At least there he would be able to put his restless energy to some use.

"Are you ready to put the star on?"

Amanda turned and stared at the decoration in Matthew's hands. She pretended she was transfixed by the glittering eleven-point Bethlehem star she'd managed to sneak out of her parents' house before she'd taken that final walk of shame out of their lives.

She'd been the only one who really enjoyed decorating the Christmas tree anyhow, she'd justified at the time. Now it was a little part of her family history for her son. She'd tell him one day. Just as she would tell him about Matthew.

He'd been his usual charming self when he'd accepted her invitation to enjoy some mince pies and help decorate the tree, but ever since he'd arrived his natural warmth had been tinged with a slightly squirrely edge she couldn't put a finger on. Maybe she should have offered him the spare room last night. Not that she would have been able to sleep, knowing there was six-foot-something of sexy down the corridor.

Ugh. This was a no-win situation. Why couldn't she have gotten pregnant by someone she wasn't in love with?

Wait.

What?

"Amanda? What do you want?"

She looked up at Matthew, confused as to what he was asking about. A life of wedded bliss? *Yup.* She'd go for that.

"The star? Are you ready for the star?" He wiggled it in her eyeline, obscuring his baby blues.

Oh. Christmas tree. Son. Responsibility.

"Sure." She pulled back and gave her shoulders a little up-down shake before turning to Tristan, who was still busily hanging tiny shatterproof baubles along the lower branches of what had turned out to be a ridiculously beautiful tree. "Tristan, darling. Would you like to watch the Christmas star light up?"

She took a few steps back and sat cross-legged on

the floor, pulling her little boy into her lap and wrapping her arms around him as Matthew made a show of trying to reach the top of the tree and failing, much to Tristan's delight.

Thank heavens Matthew's attention was focused on their son. She was flustered and light-headed as her heart and brain met somewhere in the middle and had a discussion. She was in love with Matthew. The dedicated bachelor who hadn't been able to wait to get out through the front door last night. Who had reluctantly agreed to come over today. Who didn't want to be a part of their lives.

She watched Matthew stretch to his full length, his shirt and jumper rucking up enough for her to get a glimpse of the stomach she vividly remembered skidding her fingers across, her body growing more taut with desire at each touch.

"Look good?" he asked.

"Perfect," she whispered, only to be caught off guard as Matthew turned around.

When their eyes met her breath caught in her throat. He'd seen the look in her eyes. The longing. The burning ache for his touch. Their gazes clashed with a burst of fire that ignited and turned from innocent ogling to scorching desire in an instant.

"Star!"

Tristan began clapping his hands—a welcome distraction from the hunger she hadn't expected to feel. The bone-deep yearning for all of this to be real.

And then the doorbell rang.

"Don't worry, darlings," Florence trilled from the doorway, precariously balancing a tray of mince pies in one hand. "I'll get it."

Matthew shot Amanda a questioning look and she

shrugged, still reeling from the potency of her feelings for him. She hadn't invited anyone.

The second the door opened an exchange of "Merry Christmases" floated into the entryway and into the sitting room Amanda's heart went still. Icicles of insecurity replaced the warmth and comfort of the afternoon they'd just shared together.

Frozen in place, she found it impossible to turn around. Move. Blink, even. What were *they* doing here?

Tristan looked up at her with the same questioning gaze she could feel Matthew sending from across the room.

What's going on? Why have these strangers turned you white as the snow?

"Amanda, darling!" Florence's slightly anxious voice called out from the doorway. "Look who's popped in for a mince pie and some mulled wine!"

Amanda helped Tristan to his feet and pushed herself up to stand. Avoiding Matthew's pure blue eyes, she turned around, willing her lips into a smile as her eyes lit on the new arrivals.

"Mum. Dad. Happy Christmas!"

Matthew was no expert on family relations, but even *he* could see that Florence had engineered this situation and relied upon the sheer Britishness of everyone in the room to at the very least kick things off on a civilized foot.

A very well-heeled foot, from the looks of things.

Amanda's parents oozed the kind of wealth that only came from generations of elevated comfort and privilege. Her father shrugged off one of Savile Row's latest winter coats and handed it to Florence as if she were little more than a servant. Or perhaps it was just a sign of the nerves everyone was feeling.

"Oh, dear. I hope we've not come too early," said Amanda's mother.

Violet, was it? Her eyes darted from Amanda to Matthew and then stopped, transfixed by the little boy who was brave enough to walk over to the newcomers.

"Tristan," he said, pointing to his chest.

He handed his grandmother a bauble, then took her by the hand and led her over to the tree.

"Oh, goodness. Well, hello there." Violet Wakehurst's expression switched from anxious to enchanted and then back again, as if her features were being spun like a pinwheel, clearly unable to choose how she actually felt. "Would you like me to put this—? Oh, are you seeing this, Giles, darling? All right, we'll put it on this branch, here, shall we?"

Matthew watched Violet's fingers, trembling ever so slightly, as she hung the ornament on the tree, looked down at her grandson, then at her husband, and finally to her daughter, with astonishment and pleasure lighting up her features in equal measure.

How did he do it? Matthew shook his head in wonder. How did this little boy win over the grandmother he'd never met in the same way he'd reached into his own heart?

The answer came to him in an instant.

Faith.

The faith of an innocent believing that all would be right in the world as long as there was love. It was instinctual. In the same way survival was. Instinct was guiding Tristan to bring them all together.

"What brings you two here? Bedford Square isn't on your usual round of Christmas parties." Amanda's eyes flashed from parent to parent.

The look she threw Matthew was so fast he almost

missed it, but its intensity made an impact. Her whole body language was that of a frightened child. There was a brittle edge to her voice he hadn't heard before. Self-preservation, he thought, glancing at Tristan. Amanda was acting from the other end of the emotional spectrum…as an adult who had taught herself that trust, faith and belief weren't her allies. Couldn't be relied on to carry her through a situation she had never envisaged.

The father of her child and her estranged parents were in the room, with the son she had vowed to protect.

In her shoes he would have run to the sink to throw cold water on his face. Rouse himself from what *had* to be a nightmare.

"I invited them, love. 'tis the season and all that!" Florence brightly cut through the thick atmosphere in the room. "Mince pie, anyone?" She swirled the plate round the room, sending her brother's coat flying off to the sofa. No one moved. "Oh, heavens! Where are my manners? Matthew." She gave him a warm smile. "I believe you have met my brother Giles and his wife Violet before. At a charity event, was it? Something about soldiers?"

Florence's intervention softened things. Gave the uncomfortable group some chitchat to get them through the awkwardness of the scenario.

After a few exchanges of, "Oh, yes, I remember," or, "It was at the Savoy, wasn't it, darlings?" and, "Weren't you also at the SoS benefit, Amanda?" the cool conversational temperature begin to warm. A touch.

"Here." Matthew decided to take the bull by the horns and stepped across to shake Amanda's parents' hands. "Shall I take your coats? Give you a chance to get comfortable?"

Amanda shot him a horrified *Don't leave me alone*

look, counterbalanced by Florence interjection as she wrapped an arm around her niece's shoulders.

"That's a wonderful suggestion, Matthew, dear. And while you're at it would you mind awfully nipping into the kitchen and fetching the mulled wine? I've set out some porcelain mugs next to the range."

"Of course." Matthew nodded, wondering if this was actually his cue to absent himself from the house all together or just Florence orchestrating an opportunity for them to explain his presence.

As he began ladling the spiced wine into the delicate mugs he heard the door swoosh open behind him.

"How could you *do* that?" Amanda raged, as much as she could in a whisper.

"What? I was doing what your aunt asked." Matthew feigned innocence.

"Don't be ridiculous. Were you part of this? Did you help her bring them here?"

If Matthew hadn't known the steam coming from behind Amanda's head was from the mulled wine he would have sworn it was coming from her head. Despite the intensity of Amanda's fury, he laughed.

She punched him in the arm. "What are you laughing for? This is a total nightmare! *You!*" She jabbed him in the chest with a finger. *"My parents!"* She flicked her thumb toward the sitting room, then pulled herself taut and growled, "They're in there with your son. Would you bloody *do* something about it?"

Matthew couldn't help himself. He laughed again.

Not ten minutes ago he had been wondering if he was welcome, and now Amanda was asking him to leap into the saddle and go into battle on behalf of her and their son.

"Why. Are. You. *Laughing*?" Amanda demanded, her cheeks pinkening with barely contained fury.

Matthew put the ladle down and rubbed his hands along her arms, even more amused when she stiffened in his touch like a little wooden toy soldier.

"C'mon, love. This is all a bit ridiculous, isn't it? This whole set-up? I have to give it to your Auntie Florence. She doesn't do things by halves, does she?"

Amanda's fury seemed to double. "She has gone well and truly over the top this time. First she makes me invite you to Winter Wonderland, then she insists you come along with the tree, using Tristan and making Christmas memories as—"

"Wait a minute." All the warmth dropped from his voice. "What are you talking about, *made* you invite me? You didn't want me to be part of this? Get to know my own son?"

"No." Amanda balled her hands into fists as if grabbing back all the words she wanted to say but wouldn't. "That wasn't it at all."

"Well?" Matthew asked, after she'd glared at him without any sign of throwing some light onto the matter. "Why don't we break this down? Are you venting at me because you're angry with your aunt, or are you angry at me for showing up in your life?"

"Noooo!" Amanda's eyes shone with tears as the word scraped the length of her throat. "Of course I want you here—it's all I've ever—" She stopped, her fingers flying to cover her mouth.

"All you've ever what? Wanted? Because if that's what you were going to say I can tell you right here, right now, without having had a single sip of your aunt's intensely boozy mulled wine, that I feel the exact same way. And I'm prepared to go a step further. Call it madness, call it destiny—call it the Auntie Florence Effect—but I'm in love with you, Amanda Wakehurst. And if you don't want to deal with your parents alone you don't have to."

"I don't understand." Amanda was shaking her head in disbelief. "What are you saying?"

"Beyond the simple fact that I love you?" Matthew looked up and scratched his head.

He hadn't planned on saying any of it, but now that he'd told her he was prepared to take any steps, go to any lengths, to ensure she and Tristan were happy and provided for. Including taking one on the chin from her parents.

"How about this…?" He crossed to her and pulled her hands into his, held them to his lips, dropping kisses on each of them. "Why don't we go back in there and tell everyone we're sorry about any confusion, but the real reason we've all come together today is for an engagement party?"

Amanda's fingers went limp in his hands, and shadows instead of sparks of joy darkened her eyes.

She tugged her hands out of his and began shaking her head back and forth. *No, no, no.*

"I'm sorry, Matthew. I can't do that. Put all that burden on you. I can see what you're doing, and it is so generous and unbelievably kind of you, but I cannot accept your offer."

Matthew flinched at her refusal, but knew he'd just thrown more fuel on a fire that was in danger of combusting. He could hardly take the proposal back, and was astonished to discover he didn't want to. So he did the only thing he could think of. He pulled Amanda into his arms and began to kiss her.

The first kiss was soft. So gentle it was just a brush of the lips. "Tell me you don't love me too," he murmured, before pressing his lips to hers again. He felt her body melt a little in his arms, her fingertips press against his chest. "Just tell me you don't love me too and I will do whatever you say."

He nuzzled into the crook between her chin and her throat, kissing and caressing and murmuring with all the tenderness he hadn't known was living in his heart.

"Anything?" Amanda pressed away from him, tears openly pouring down her cheeks.

"Of course, love. I'd do anything for you and Tristan."

She swiped at her cheeks and steeled herself after taking a step or two back. "I can't marry you."

A lacerating sting of pain swept through him, but he refused to let her look away. He took two steps toward her and cupped her face in his hands, ignoring her rigid shoulders, her cheeks taut with the breath held in her chest as if it were her only lifeline.

"Can't or won't?"

"Both, if that's what it takes!"

"Amanda, darling— Oh! Sorry, luvvies, I…" Florence had whirled into the kitchen and was mid-about-face when she realized she *wasn't* interrupting a romantic tryst. "Matthew? What are you—? Amanda, dear, come here."

She tugged Amanda toward her while Matthew's hands dropped to his sides.

"What in heaven's name is going on? I know I was being a bit of a rascal, inviting your parents here, but…" Florence dropped any pretense of trying to understand the scenario and opted for her old-world upbringing. "Let's just get this mulled wine out there, shall we? Or a cup of tea? Shall I put the kettle on? Amanda, darling, you are looking awfully pale. I'm so sorry. I know I should've told you first—"

"No, Auntie Florence. It's all right."

Amanda shook her head, her complexion so pale it made Matthew's heart ache.

"It wasn't you—"

"I was trying to ask your bullheaded niece to marry me," Matthew finally bit out, unable to bear the building tension any longer. "It seems I may have jumped the gun. Or pulled open the wrong advent calendar door. Either way…" He briskly swiped his hands together and rubbed them against the outsides of his thighs. "I'll be off. Give Tristan a good-night kiss for me, would you?"

He aimed the request at Amanda, knowing his voice dripped with venom.

"If it isn't too much bother," he continued. "See you at the hospital no doubt. All the best, Florence."

He dropped a polite kiss on her soft cheek and gave her arm a squeeze before walking out of the kitchen, grabbing his coat off the wooden stand, and closing the door behind him with a finality that even *he* believed.

A romance over before it had even begun.

He should have trusted his instinct from the first. He wasn't the man Amanda wanted. He was damaged goods and destined to be alone.

CHAPTER FOURTEEN

"TRISTAN'S FATHER?" HER parents repeated in tandem, as if they hadn't quite heard her.

Amanda nodded, lips pressed tight, her eyes anxiously darting up to the ceiling even though she knew Tristan was listening to story after story from Auntie Florence.

"Well, that's wonderful, darling, isn't it?" her mother asked.

"What is? Now that you know Tristan's father is rich? Titled? Which is it? Or is it that he's a doctor as well as being Sir Matthew Chase."

She knew she was lashing out at her parents when she should be pummeling herself. And each of the things she was naming were superficial trappings. It wasn't the title, the job or the money that interested her. It was the man.

Matthew Chase.

With his blue eyes and his dark chocolate hair and his surprisingly warm heart she knew she'd only just seen glimpses of him, with so much more yet to reveal. Each and every centimeter of him was…*perfect*. She loved him. And she'd just sent him away.

Just saying his name filled her with the deep ache of loss. How had she made such a mess of things? *Again*.

The answer was a bitter pill to swallow. She always

ruined things. It was why she'd sent him away. She'd been expediting the inevitable.

But why did it feel so bone-achingly awful? As if she'd cut off a limb from her own body?

"Amanda, I wasn't saying *any* of those things," her mother bit out. "We are just delighted to know that Tristan's father is in his life."

"Well, he isn't anymore," Amanda retorted, vividly aware that she was fast-track regressing to being the petulant teenager her parents had been so thrilled to send away to boarding school.

She closed her eyes against her mother and father's shocked expression and willed herself to be still…waiting…listening…finally hearing the steady *thump-thump* of her heart. She wasn't that petulant teen anymore. It was time to be the woman she'd always hoped she would become.

"For today, you mean? Has he left to go to the hospital?" her mother prompted.

"No. Not exactly."

"What do you mean 'not exactly'?" her father asked, his eyes narrowing in an all too familiar echo of her childhood.

"I mean he was here to spend time with Tristan. With both of us. And…and now he isn't."

She dropped her head into her hands and stemmed the deep, low moan building in her gut.

What had she done?

She knew this collision of past and present had been a long time coming—she just hadn't expected it to come with a proposal! How she had found the power to say no was beyond her. A no that was beginning to make less and less sense with each passing minute.

Lifting her head and forcing herself to face her parents—look them straight in the eye—she took the step she knew she had needed to take for a while. Years, really.

"Mum? Dad? I need your help."

She held up her hands, wanting to finish what she was saying before they leapt in with their usual admonishments about not managing her money properly, getting pregnant without being in a solid relationship.

"I know there are a lot of ways I could have conducted myself—over my whole life, really—that would have made you more proud of me..." She held her hands out to her sides. "But this is who I am. I am filled with flaws. I act impetuously. And my actions...they have ramifications. Believe me when I say I have been carrying around the guilt about John's death for years. I know it's my fault—"

"Amanda, love..." her father gently cut in. "That's not true."

"Of course it's true! I told him he needed to pull his weight. To sign up for another tour. It's my fault he went back to Afghanistan. It's my fault he's dead."

"No." Both her parents were shaking their heads now, their expressions soft. Compassionate, even. "Any disagreement the two of you were having didn't back John into a corner."

Amanda's brow crinkled. "What are you talking about? How would *you* know?"

"We met with John's parents a few years ago," her mother explained. "When we heard what had happened in Afghanistan."

"They met with you?"

"Yes, well..." Her father's lips thinned, then parted as he continued. "We offered to help pay for John's funeral and were refused. Emotions were running high, as you can imagine. So we thought we would wait a while and then approach them to see if there was a charity we could donate to in John's name."

Amanda stared wide-eyed at her parents. Had they tried to make amends for a man's death with *money*?

"Giles, just go on and tell her everything."

"I don't understand why you're telling me *any* of this," Amanda bristled. "It was thirteen years ago. Why come to me now and dig up the past? An incredibly *painful* past I have worked hard to put behind me."

She looked between her parents until her father finally laced his hands together between his knees and began speaking.

"What we're trying to say, Amanda, is that you aren't the only one who has made their share of mistakes. We're all muddling through, and with things so—so tense between us…"

Her mother pressed a tissue to her lips, trying to stem a small sob.

Her father's expression turned remorseful. "We haven't exactly been on talking terms, have we, darling?"

Amanda squirmed at the term of endearment. Virtually ten years of being ostracized by them had taken its toll.

It would be so easy to jump up from the sofa and walk out on them the way they had walked out on her when she'd told them she was pregnant with Tristan.

But there was another, louder side of her heart that badly wanted to be her parents' little girl again. Their darling daughter. If she could overcome those years of hurt in an instant she would run across to the sofa, drop to her knees and hug them both, weep and sob for sending Matthew away and, while she was at it, weep some more for all the mistakes she had made before.

But they weren't that type of family.

So she did what she always did—shook her head and braced herself for the latest catalogue of disappointments she'd weighted the Wakehurst history books with this time.

Her father gruffly cleared his throat and began again. "As I said, we tracked John's parents down, hoping to make a donation to a charity in his name—"

"What? To make amends for your daughter sending him to his death?"

Amanda hated herself for sounding so bitter about the gesture—so *angry*—but she wasn't a little girl anymore. *She* was the one who had to accept responsibility for John's death. Not have her parents sneaking around salving wounds in the only way they knew how—with money.

"Well, no, as it turns out. It wasn't that at all."

Amanda scrubbed her hands through her hair. "What do you mean?"

"John had always been signed up to go on another tour."

Ice ran through her veins. That hadn't been what he'd said. He'd blamed it all on her. On the trust fund drying up. Her refusal to leave medical school.

Her father said, "He didn't want to return, which was fairly understandable, but his parents insisted he make good on his commitment to the military. To honor his promises."

Amanda's whole body began to hum with discord. "You mean he didn't go solely because of me?"

"According to his parents, he finally agreed to go because he was ashamed of the way he'd treated you and didn't know how to come clean, as it were." Her father looked down at his hands again before continuing. "He sent them a letter when he arrived in Afghanistan. It explained everything."

"What did it say?" Amanda managed to choke out the words, covering her face with her hands as if that would shield her from the truth.

For the last thirteen years she'd been living with the guilt of John's death. She had believed that she was responsible for a soldier going into battle against his will.

"He took responsibility for everything."

Amanda sat upright, her hands falling to her lap, her jaw following in their wake. "What do you mean, 'everything'? What could he have taken responsibility for?"

"He said he and his army mates had overheard you and your friends having dinner when you were in Las Vegas. It had become clear to them that the three of you were comfortably off and that your positions in society were…were more *fortunate* than his own."

Her father swiped a hand across his face and his wife reached out to put her hand on his knee.

"What is it?" Amanda demanded. "What aren't you telling me?"

"It was a dare!" her father blurted. "The whole thing was a dare. The wedding…trying to move up a social tier at your expense…the entire thing was a bet."

Amanda sat entirely motionless, replaying the words she'd swear she'd just heard coming out of her father's mouth.

A dare?

Amanda was speechless. She'd never really known what feeling completely stunned felt like until now. Maybe thunderstruck was a better word.

Slowly at first, then at a rate of knots she could barely keep up with, everything shifted into place.

From the moment they'd landed back in the UK John

had been strange. He'd gone from being completely adoring to barely touching her—except in that one violent exchange. If his parents had known all along what he'd done... No wonder they had been awkward around her.

All these years she'd thought they had been blaming her, when they had actually been blaming their son! Trying to get him to come clean. How awful for them to lose him to war before they'd had a chance to make their peace. No wonder...

Her heart softened as she looked across the room to the sofa where her parents sat, their expressions anxious, their hands woven together as if sending energy from one to the other. Her parents had been trying to help her all along. Even if it had been impossible to divine as they muddled on in their own awkward, gentrified, super-British stiff-upper-lip way.

"So that's why you hosted the SoS event?" Amanda finally said.

They nodded in tandem. It struck Amanda how much of a unit her parents were. There wasn't a slip of paper thin enough to wedge between the pair of them. Not physically, of course, but they were the most happily, solidly married couple she had ever known.

Her mother crossed and then re-crossed her legs as she went through the motions of choosing how to tell the next part of the story.

"We were going to tell you after the event...a day or so later. But then you disappeared, and we thought being amongst all those soldiers had made everything worse instead of better, so we thought we'd leave it a couple of weeks. Then when we did meet and heard your news..."

"You didn't know how to tell me that the last ten years of my life had been a joke?" Amanda finished for her.

Her mother nodded, tears cascading down her cheeks.

"We're so sorry, Amanda. We responded so poorly, and we know how passionate you can be—"

"You mean foolhardy?" Amanda interjected.

"No. Of course not. You give your full heart to everything. First medicine and now Tristan."

"How do you know anything about Tristan?" Amanda's back stiffened defensively.

"Florence has been keeping us up to date with everything at our request. She's very protective of you, but your father can't get enough pictures of Tristan. With those blue eyes he's so like—" She stopped abruptly and pressed her fingers to her mouth.

"So like his father?" Amanda finished for her.

Her mother nodded. "If you'd like to try again…if you can trust us…we'd love so very much to try and make up for lost time."

"With Tristan?"

"With both of you." Her father opened his hands to Amanda. "We know we have made a complete and utter hash of being your parents. But if you're willing to give us another chance we'd love to try and make up for it."

"How do you feel about starting right now?"

Quizzical expressions shot on to her parents' faces as they watched their daughter jump from the sofa.

"Would you be all right to help Auntie Florence with Tristan? I think I've made one of the worst mistakes of my life and I need to go fix it."

"So…you're—you're happy for us to be with Tristan? Be in your home?"

"Of course I am!" Amanda crossed to them and gave them each a kiss on the cheek. "I know it's going to take some getting used to—for all of us—but if I don't go now I might turn the rest of my life into one more cruel joke. I've got to go. For Tristan."

Her parents pulled her into a tight hug, then ushered her out into the corridor, insisting she bundle herself up against the thick snowfall blanketing London.

"Where are you going?" her father asked as she pulled the door open.

"To the hospital!"

And with her heart thumping against her rib cage she ran out through the door and across the square to find the one man she prayed would find a way to forgive her. To make this Christmas miracle complete.

CHAPTER FIFTEEN

"DR. CHASE, WE really are properly staffed tonight." Dr. McBride stood, arms crossed, as if protecting the assignment board from Matthew. "Thank you for seeing to the last couple of patients, but I think your energies might be better spent..." he looked up to the ceiling to search for words "...finding your Zen."

"Rubbish. I don't even know what that means."

"It means..." Dr. McBride reinserted himself between Matthew and the assignment board "...you look like you need a day off."

"When's the last time *you* had a day off? You're always knackered."

Matthew knew he was being childish. Knew Dr. McBride was making the best call both for the rest of the staff and the patients. He'd stormed into the hospital like a wounded pterodactyl, prepared to blame the world for the heart that was breaking into pieces inside his chest.

He had yanked on a white coat. Insisted on seeing the worst cases. Elbowed in on cases already being tended to. He was acting like a first-class boor. And none of it was making him feel any better.

"Things are running smoothly tonight," Dr. McBride continued gently. "We'll be all right if you head home."

Home? As if he knew where *that* was. Home was with

Amanda and Tristan. He knew it was complete madness, but being with them had meant feeling whole again for the very first time since Charlie had died. Like a man. A father. Someone worthy of love. It was devastating him that he would never feel that way again.

He stared at Dr. McBride willing him to have mercy on a man who wanted, *needed*, to prove his worth.

"Since when does this hospital run smoothly?" Matthew shifted from side to side, trying to get a glimpse at the board.

"Since you and Dr. Wakehurst came to work here," Dr. McBride answered kindly.

He was obviously reading Matthew's high-octane vibes for what they were. A man with energy to burn, minus the exacting focus he needed to attend to patients. Minus the empathy, more like. The care. The compassion he'd vowed to give each and every patient the day he had decided to become a doctor. The day his brother had died.

"It's almost Christmas Eve, Dr. Chase. That's when things tend to get crazier. I really do suggest you go on home—or why not go out and do some Christmas shopping?"

The words struck Matthew like a dagger in the chest. His brother would be alive today if his parents hadn't gone ruddy Christmas shopping. Or if he'd listened when his brother had asked him to stop playing video games for a few minutes. To talk.

Why hadn't he taken the time?

Dr. McBride reached out a hand as if to turn Matthew toward the exit. Why was everyone blocking his efforts to help? All he wanted to do was *work*, for heaven's sake!

"I really am going to have to pull rank here—"

"I don't think you can do that unless I'm around as well."

Amanda's voice lanced straight through his chest like the hot swipe of a blade through butter. "It's still a job share."

Slowly he turned around, acutely aware that Dr. McBride was inching out of his peripheral vision and away from the pair of them. He knew he was sending out growly monster vibes, but Amanda... She was...she was positively *glowing*. Snowflakes were turning to dewdrops on her hair. Her cheeks were flushed. She was breathing rapidly, as if she'd run there.

"Where's Tristan?" he asked, feeling too raw to ask what she was doing here. "Is something wrong?"

"He's fine. Asleep, if Auntie Florence's storytelling was up to her usual par."

"I thought your parents were there?"

"They were. *Are*," she corrected, still smiling. "They said they'd wait until I got back in case Florence needed anything."

He arched an eyebrow. "All fences mended, then? How nice for you. A lovely tableau of Christmas magic playing out in Bedford Square."

Amanda nodded, her mood completely unaffected by his verbal lashings.

"Do you know if any of the family rooms are free?" she asked, her eyes twinkling.

"Hardly appropriate for us, don't you think?"

Matthew hated the sharpness of his tone and—finally!—the tight wince of Amanda's response, but what could she possibly want from him now that she'd made it clear she didn't want him in her life?

"I made a mistake," she said, without embellishment.

"We *all* make mistakes, love. No need to run across here to remind me just how badly I misjudged the situation."

He'd started to turn away when Amanda laid a hand on his arm and lowered her voice.

"Please. Matthew. The mistake was mine. Can we go to one of the family rooms and talk?"

From her firm stance—hands on hips, head cocked to one side—it looked as if it was the only way he'd get her out of his hair.

He wanted to say no with every pore in his body. But something deep within him was rattling his cage.

If you leave things this way you will probably never see Amanda and Tristan again.

And then it hit him. Charlie had thought there was no way out. No one to speak to. No one to help him try and understand what he was going through. No one he could go to for help. Not even his little brother.

But Amanda was *here*. She was trying. She might not be planning to say things he wanted to hear, but the least he could do was hear her out. Take the chance that they could have a civil relationship and perhaps let him be a father to his son.

"Fine." He gestured toward a corridor off to the left. "I think the end room is free."

When they entered the room he waited for her to sit down before sitting in a stiff chair across from her. He held up a hand when she began to speak and began, as neutrally as he could, "I owe you an explanation."

"No, you don't." Amanda's ponytail swung from shoulder to shoulder as she shook her head.

"I do," Matthew insisted. Strongly enough that she tightened her lips and made a zipping gesture in front of them. "I'm sure you've seen hints that I'm not…that I didn't come out of my teens unscathed either."

Amanda sat on her hands as he continued. He almost

smiled at the gesture, knowing it was her way of stopping herself from interrupting.

"When I was a teenager my brother Charlie—he was much older than me... I was a late 'surprise.' Anyway, he was in the army. He came back from Kosovo pretty messed up. *Very* messed up. My parents didn't really know what to do, so they did what all good British parents do and just battled on through, keeping a stiff upper lip."

Amanda nodded. He could see in her eyes that she knew exactly what he was talking about. It gave him the courage to continue.

"A few months after he was given leave for depression, my parents asked me to keep an eye on him while they went out and did some Christmas shopping. I was a teenager. Obsessed with gaming. It was the only way I related to Charlie, but since he'd come back he'd had no interest in the games—particularly the ones that involved shooting. He couldn't bear it. I forced him to sit in on a game with me, trying to make good on my promise to my parents. He excused himself. Said something about the attic. But it didn't registered. I thought he'd gone to the kitchen for a cup of tea...some biscuits..."

He looked into Amanda's eyes, feeling such shame for what had happened. If only he had followed him. Turned on the television instead of playing those ridiculous games!

He continued tonelessly. "I found him about twenty minutes later... By the time I got him down from the rope it was too late to revive him."

"Oh, Matthew..."

Amanda's voice was little more than a whisper. But instead of looking repulsed, disgusted, as she rightly should be, her expression was one of pure compassion.

She reached out her hands to him. "I am so sorry you had to go through that."

"Don't be. It wasn't your fault. It was mine. It's time I owned it."

"What do you mean? I am *so* sorry you lost your brother, and the circumstances sound heartbreaking, but it wasn't your fault. And just think of all the lives you have saved with SoS."

"It never seems to be enough." His voice cracked and for the first time he didn't edit himself. Didn't cover up the anguish he had lived with for so long. "None of it will ever bring Charlie back. None of it will make my family whole again."

Amanda considered him for a moment, then stood up and moved to the chair next to him, placing her hand on his. "What if you made a new family?"

Despite himself, Matthew gave a sad laugh. "We've been through that. I was being ridiculous. Too bloody headstrong, as usual."

Amanda pulled back with an indignant huff. "If your idea of being 'bloody headstrong' means founding an extraordinary charity, being an amazing doctor, saving lives in war zones and fathering the most perfect little boy in the whole of Britain, I shall spend all my days bragging about my *bloody headstrong* husband."

Matthew stared at her for a minute. "Husband?"

Amanda's shoulders scrunched up to her ears as her face turned into an apologetic wince. "Which would make me your wife… Unless you've changed your mind?"

"You want to marry me?" He gave his head a shake and looked at her again. "Even though—?"

She pressed a finger to his lips. "Even though *nothing*. Whatever happened in your past has made you the man you are today. I learnt that about myself today, too. Just now, in fact."

She laughed, as if it were the most madcap epiphany

she'd ever had, then softened her features, pinning him with the most loving look he'd ever been on the receiving end of.

"I am so sorry you had to live through such heartache to get where you are today, but because of it you're one of the most inspirational, incredible men I have ever met. So much so," she added, with a coquettish note to her voice, "that I am almost certain I've fallen completely in love with you."

"Almost?"

"Definitely." She gave a sharp nod, as if cementing the fact.

Amanda was in love him.

A warm wash of heat surrounded Matthew's heart, and before he could allow another moment for either of them to change their minds again he stood up and pulled her into his arms.

"I think you'll find you've had the same effect on me."

"The dizzy, weak-kneed, all-I-want-to-do-is-kiss-you effect?" Amanda asked through a grin as wide as the Cheshire cat's.

"That one," Matthew agreed, lowering his lips to meet hers, a kiss being the only way to acknowledge his love for his future wife properly. "And long may it continue."

He dipped his head further, until their lips met and flared with the heated passion of a couple who had just begun a journey they knew they no longer had to make alone.

With this woman by my side, Matthew thought as their kisses deepened and the ice in his heart at long last began to thaw, *I will do everything in my power to make the world a better place.*

CHAPTER SIXTEEN

"IT'S TIME FOR the star!" Tristan clapped his hands, then went round to the small rug where his little sister was practicing her newly acquired walking skills in her bright-eyed, eighteen-month-old way. "Look, Immi! Daddy's putting on the star!"

Matthew smiled and tousled his son's hair. "What would you say if Daddy picked Mummy up and let *her* put the star on the tree?"

He took Amanda by the hand and twirled her into his arms as if they were dancers in a Hollywood musical.

Amanda nestled into her husband's arms, then pulled back a smidgen. "Oops—not too tight. I don't want to hurt you with the star."

"Hurt me?" Matthew put on a look of shocked disbelief. "Never."

"Can everything stay exactly as it is tonight?" Amanda looked into his eyes, sure the love in her heart was shining through them to her husband.

"Not even to practice ways of giving Immi a little sister or brother to tease the way Tristan teases her?"

Amanda quirked an eyebrow at him. "Mmm… I suppose I could be persuaded to practice—so long as you're happy to be a father of three a bit sooner than anticipated."

"What?" Matthew's eyes widened. "Are you saying what I think you're saying?"

Amanda nodded, her eyes bright as she went up on tiptoe and gave Matthew a soft kiss before whispering, "Someone who looks a lot like you is going to be a daddy again in nine months."

"Mummy! Daddy!" Tristan pointed toward the top of the tree to remind them of what they were meant to be doing.

Matthew dipped down and wrapped his arms around Amanda's legs. He lifted her up so her eyes were level with the top of the tree. She held out the star and was about to put it on when she turned to Matthew and Tristan.

"What do we say when we put the star on the tree?" she asked.

Matthew smiled up at Amanda, and together the three of them chorused, "It's time for a Christmas miracle!"

As Matthew loosened his grip on Amanda's legs she slid down until her toes touched the floor. He tugged her in tight. "You know *you're* my miracle, don't you, love?"

"Even though I put my cold feet on you every night?"

"It wouldn't be bedtime without them."

Matthew smiled, before standing back and giving Amanda's belly a proud rub. He turned her and wrapped his arms around her as they enjoyed the twinkling luster of the newly decorated tree.

Amanda couldn't believe how different her life was, only three years on from that fateful day she'd gone for an interview at Bankside Hospital.

She gave Matthew's arms a squeeze and leant back against his chest, knowing in her heart that she was enjoying all the Christmas miracles she needed…

And this year she prayed that someone else would feel the joy she felt at that very moment.

* * * * *

MILLS & BOON®

MEDICAL ROMANCE™

THE ULTIMATE IN ROMANTIC MEDICAL DRAMA

217/03

MILLS & BOON®

EXCLUSIVE EXTRACT

One sizzling encounter with trauma doc Major Elle
Caplin is all it takes to tempt Lieutenant Colonel
Fitzwilliam to break his one-night rule…!

Read on for a sneak preview of
TEMPTED BY DR OFF-LIMITS
the second book in Charlotte Hawkes's
HOT ARMY DOCS *duet*

Fitz forgot everything. He simply indulged. For what
seemed like an eternity, his mouth slid over hers. When he
pushed, she pushed back. When he held back, Elle sought
him. He trailed kisses down her jaw, her collarbone and to
the hollow at the base of her neck. Her shivers of pleasure
stoked his need. And each time he returned to those plump,
pink lips, her mouth reached for his and her tongue met
his in the same sinfully sinuous dance.

As he gave himself up to the sensations, as each kiss
from Elle threatened to undermine every defence he'd spent
years putting in place, the plink of those warm droplets on
his ice-block heart growing more insistent.

Before he could help himself, he'd released the curtain
of reds and golds from its military bun, inhaling its familiar
fresh, floral scent as his hands buried themselves in its
luxuriant depths. He could recall exactly how it had felt
brushing over his naked skin that night and his body
tightened.

'Gabrielle,' he groaned, unable to make up his mind
whether it was a groan or a warning growl.

And still he kissed her, sometimes gently and reverently,
other times hard and greedily. As though he never wanted
to stop. He didn't know when he backed her up so that she

was sitting on his desk with him standing between her legs, or when his fingers crept under the hem of her tee, or when he lifted it over her head and dropped it in a puddle on the plans he was supposed to be going through.

He needed to stop. Needed to remind her—remind himself—what kind of a man he was. How he would inevitably hurt her.

Don't miss HOT ARMY DOCS:
ENCOUNTER WITH A COMMANDING OFFICER
Available now!

TEMPTED BY DR OFF-LIMITS
Available January 2018!
www.millsandboon.co.uk